ROWAN: FIREBRAND COWBOYS

BARB HAN

TORJAKE PUBLISHING

Copyright © 2023 by Barb Han

All rights reserved.

No part of this book may be reproduced in any form or by any electronic or mechanical means, including information storage and retrieval systems, without written permission from the author, except for the use of brief quotations in a book review.

Editing: Ali Williams

Cover Design: Jacob's Cover Designs

Proofreading: Judicious Revisions

To Brandon, Jacob, and Tori for being the great loves of my life. To Babe for being my hero, my best friend, and my place to call home.

1

Rowan Firebrand's world wasn't going to hell in a handbasket. No. A handbasket would be far too smooth a ride. A handbasket would be way too slow. His world was going to hell in a racecar at a hundred-and-thirty-miles-per-hour while careening out of control. There were no bumpers or hay bales strong enough to keep this hot mess from flying off the track and diving headfirst into the fire.

A chill in the late-February air reminded Rowan that he was in Colorado, not Texas. The Rio Grande National Forest, with its millions of acres, was far enough away from anyone or anything named Firebrand. This solo trip was his best chance to recalibrate and, maybe, find a little peace. Between his mother being in the hospital after surviving a jail fight—don't get him started on how messed up that sounded even to him—and all the other drama surrounding his family and the cattle ranch, he'd needed to get the heck out of Dodge in a manner of speaking. It was impossible to think clearly back home. A change of pace was needed or he would lose his mind.

At one point did life get so messed up?

Rowan glanced up at the gathering clouds, figured he had an hour, maybe two before the weather would turn ugly. It would be nice to have his camping spot set up by the time it hit, but that wasn't likely at this rate. After checking in with his brother Nick, he'd powered down his cell to save battery. Rowan had no idea how long he would be staying in the forest. He had enough food and supplies to last a week, more if he rationed. Plus, he could always hunt or fish when needed.

The trail ahead was uphill and rocky, but well worn. There would be no trouble navigating the path as long as visibility was good. February in Colorado could bring whiteouts, making it impossible to see your hand extended out in front of you.

Not a hundred feet in, a young couple approached as they headed down the hill and toward the parking lot. The young woman's hair was in two long braids. She had on khaki pants, a sweater, and hiking boots that looked too new to have been worn often. The young man had on a camo-colored bucket hat with drawstring, camo-colored cargo pants, and two layers of t-shirts. Neither wore coats despite having on scarves and gloves. They looked like locals who hiked these trails when the sun was out.

"Hey," Camo Guy said as they neared each other. "You're headed the wrong direction."

"How is it up there?" Rowan asked, making polite conversation. He could no longer see the snow-covered mountain tops due to thick evergreen foliage along the winding path.

"Getting colder by the minute," Camo Guy said. His girlfriend—wife?—gave a knowing smile. "It's supposed to get bad later."

"Radar said there's a chance it might blow north of here," Rowan said as the winds picked up. A gust blasted him in the chest like a boxer might throw a punch. He zipped up his jacket in response.

"Let's hope for your sake," the good-natured Camo Guy said. He was roughly five-feet-ten-inches with a runner's build. "But the weather isn't the only problem."

"How so?" Rowan asked.

"Hungry black bears have been spotted," Camo Guy said. "There's a problem bear."

"I'll be sure to hang my food away from my camp and keep watch," Rowan said. "Thanks for the heads up."

"You sure you don't want to make a U-turn?" Camo Guy asked with a chuckle. "Might get a little rough up there. You'd hate to get stranded if we get the worst of it."

Based on his demeanor, he probably assessed Rowan as a decent-enough person who might have a screw loose for camping as a snow storm loomed.

"I'll be fine," Rowan reassured. "Do this all the time. Mother Nature hasn't taken me yet."

"Cool," Camo Guy said as he reached back for his wife or girlfriend's hand before passing by. He turned his head to the side. "Stay warm up there, and stay away from those bears."

"Will do," Rowan said before continuing the trek up the mountain. A couple holding a kid's hand passed by next, their German shepherd moving in a circle around the small family. They smiled and nodded as they went by. The German shepherd kept a wary eye on Rowan. He also took notice the dog positioned himself in between Rowan and the cherub-faced kid, who looked to be no more than three or four years old.

"Mommy, why can he stay?" the little blond boy asked when they got a few feet down the base.

"He probably forgot something up there and will be right down as soon as he finds it," the mother explained. "Everyone has to leave when the weather gets bad or risk turning into a Popsicle."

The little boy laughed.

Rowan was looking for something alright. Peace of mind. But he didn't figure this was the time to shout out his problems to strangers, no matter how tempting it was. How fast would folks run away from him the second they found out his mother had been in a jail fight? Being able to walk around without anyone knowing who he was or anything about his family was the change he needed. In Lone Star Pass, folks either stared or shot him a look of pity. He couldn't decide which was more annoying and didn't stick around to find it out.

Another group, this time five shivering teenagers, came racing down.

"Sorry," one of them yelled as he blasted past. Rowan remembered times like those with a few of his brothers or cousins. Coming from a family of nine boys, with nine male cousins, gave him more than his fair share of built-in playmates and adversaries. With recent events, the family was divided again after working hard to mend fences. There'd been more drama than any one family should have to contend with for much of his life. Thus, in part, the reason for this escape. Rowan wasn't running from the responsibility of taking care of cattle or running the ranch. He didn't need a break from calving—despite this being the prime season. He needed a break from the people. He needed time to figure out if living at Firebrand Ranch was right for him or if it was time to take the offer to move to Fort Worth and open a feed store with one of his buddies. Benny, who'd medically boarded out of the military, had made a compelling argument that it was time for a change of pace. A runner since they'd been kids, he needed to figure out how to navigate life with one leg now. His friend had read about Jackie Firebrand's arrest, and it struck him that Rowan might need a fresh start too. Or so he'd said in the voicemail he'd left, that Rowan had yet to respond to.

In the middle of all the chaos of the ranch, Rowan couldn't think clearly. Running a business was never easy. He knew the realities better than most. There'd be early mornings working the store and late nights doing the books. At first, he and Benny would have to do the lion's share of the work themselves. Rowan had family money but refused to use it. That money felt tainted since it was inherited from his grandfather, the Marshall, a man who'd spent his life dividing his sons and pitting them against each other. There were reasons behind his actions the family recently learned about. Some of the others might be able to forgive the Marshall but Rowan wasn't there yet. He may never be, which was part of the reason he was shivering his backside off right now as the wind picked up.

The higher Rowan climbed, the lower the temperature dropped. It was to be expected out here, given how altitude worked, but these dips were more extreme as the weather front blew in. He had no idea what was in store. Being prepared was key. Folks had climbed Mount Everest with the same quality of gear he had in his rucksack and survived.

The folks he'd seen coming down the mountain so far were what he would call the REI set. All their equipment was clean, matching, and brand new. Heck, if he looked closely enough he might even catch a glimpse of a tag or two still attached. If the burly mountain-looking types with their canine companions that looked more like wolves headed down, he'd worry.

Hungry bears were nothing to take lightly, though. He knew to take precautions there. Bear attacks in Colorado were on the rise. Rarely, they were fatal and he intended to keep it that way. A healthy respect for invading wildlife's territory had kept him alive for thirty-three years now. He planned to keep the streak going. A desperate bear could do a lot of damage to a person.

After hiking just shy of two hours, Rowan heard the sounds of rushing water as snow started to fall. Camping near a creek or stream would make tonight a lot easier and he needed to set up camp before the storm worsened and darkness made it impossible to see.

Staking a spot around the bend from a water source seemed like a good place. He shrugged off the rucksack before building a fire using the flint he always carried, along with tinder he'd gathered. As soon as he had a decent flame, he rubbed his cold hands together to warm them before getting to work on staking his one-person tent. Technically, he could fit two inside but they'd have to be mighty close. Not that it mattered. He traveled solo on this and many other trips and wouldn't have it any other way.

Sitting back on his heels next to the fire, he broke open a food packet of fettuccine alfredo with chicken. After gathering water in a tin cup and then boiling it over the fire, he added water to the packet. And—voila!—had a decent two-portion meal. Rowan ate both. The warmth felt good on his throat. He managed a cup of instant coffee to finish off dinner as the snow came down faster. It was late by the time he snuffed out the fire and then climbed inside his tent.

Winds whipped but the stakes held. The tent's profile

was low, built for these kinds of conditions. He toed off his boots before kicking them to the side, shrugged out of his jacket, and then climbed inside his sleeping bag. It alone would be enough to keep him warm without the tent, so the double insulation kept him downright toasty. Before zipping up and cocooning inside his Western Mountaineering Kodiak, he slipped out of his jeans and flannel shirt, leaving on his boxers, socks, and undershirt. Next to his boots, he kept a Coleman lantern and a hunting knife along with his rucksack.

Having worked thirty-six hours straight at the ranch before traveling west, he was beyond tired. Rowan bit back a yawn, turned on his side, and closed his eyes.

The sounds of splashing opened his eyes up again. Instinctively, he reached for the knife, hoping it was nothing more than his imagination or a bad dream.

He listened as the winds howled.

More splashing and an audible gasp. Or was it a bear snorting?

Rowan bit back a curse as he opened the zipper all the way and then reached for his pair of jeans. He managed to slide into them quietly as he kept his ear to the ground. Either way, he was going to have to investigate.

When he heard more splashing, he hurried up. The bear, or whatever was out there, might keep moving and not ever realize he was there. He couldn't leave this one to chance, so he unzipped enough of the tent to ease out without making any noise. He toed on his boots as he one hopped, trying to get into them while holding on to the blade and buttoning his jeans.

He heard twigs snap underneath his boots. So much for being stealthy. Being careless could get him killed.

The noise he made could scare off a bear. After all, they

tended to head the opposite direction rather than come into contact with a human. Unless they were provoked or hungry. Knowing campers were having trouble with one in this area wasn't the news he'd wanted to hear.

Rowan headed toward the sound, easing behind tree after tree for cover. The wind might have calmed down a little but the air was biting. His teeth started chattering as he zigzagged through the trees. He eased his way toward the creek until he could get a visual.

The sight froze him in his tracks. What on earth was a woman doing out here this late, looking like she was scrubbing her arms while bent over in thigh-deep water?

TARA DOWLING SAW movement out of the corner of her eye. It was ever-so-slight but something or *someone* was over behind a tree across the creek's bank. Her pulse raced and her heart thundered inside her chest. Had *he* found her? It was impossible. There was no way.

Teeth chattering, body shivering from cold, she bolted like a frightened deer with a hunter on its tail. She was too far away to get a good look at whatever was there—and beyond exhausted—but adrenaline kicked in, giving her almost superhuman speed as she raced through the trees.

She'd wanted to follow the water down to a town where she could find warmth and shelter for the night. How long had she been wandering in the forest? Half-dazed, still in shock, her flight instincts were on autopilot. The cold air blasted her skin as the temps must have dropped thirty degrees in a matter of hours.

Food. She needed something to eat before she starved.

Shelter. She needed a roof over her head.

Water. She needed to rehydrate.

Glancing down at her arms, she saw blood. *His* blood. Oh, man, how she'd needed to get that off her clothing and her skin. Speaking of clothing, her jeans and sweater weren't nearly warm enough to combat this weather. Now that they were soaked, they were heavier and much colder.

Despite believing she was running at a record-setting pace, she heard footsteps behind her. Coming closer.

"Hey," a strong male voice shouted. There was something soothing about the voice, but she knew better than to trust it. Folks could be looking for her. Bad people.

Relief nailed her at the thought it didn't belong to *him*. Maybe she was safe after all? Then again, others could be out here. Waiting. Watching.

The small cabin at the foothills of the forest was supposed to be off the grid, where he couldn't find her. Tara almost laughed out loud. He'd warned her that if she left, he wouldn't rest until she was back where she belonged. With him. And now, she'd killed a Denver cop.

If Tara lived to be a hundred, she would never understand why she'd seen him as charming when they'd first met. Then again, wasn't hindsight always perfect?

Alexander Smythe had a long reach. His cop buddies called him Xander. She nearly doubled over at the thought she could add *cop killer* to the list of names she'd been called. Xander's co-workers would see to it another name was added to the list, inmate.

The fact Tara killed her former boyfriend in self-defense wasn't something she could prove, and she doubted anyone else would come forward if she tried to make a case against him anyway. Xander had more friends and acquaintances than she did. The DA would make certain she served jail-time, causing her to lose the only person who truly mattered to her, her mom, who was presently in a rehab facility after a near-fatal car crash.

The adrenaline push depleted, Tara's legs buckled. She tucked as best she could to protect herself from the fall. Her shoulder slammed against a tree trunk on the way down. She bit out a curse.

Running away had been foolish. No one could outrun the law.

In this case, even the good cops might be too afraid of Xander's association with a criminal organization to come forward in her defense. No cop who knew him would be willing to testify against him or roll over on a fellow officer when others might hesitate to defend them when the time came, allowing a shooter to get off a shot or taking cover when they should be taking aim.

Tara knew the drill. When it came to law enforcement, loyalty to fellow officers came above personal choice. Or at least her one friend Officer Jenn McNeely had said so. If Jenn wouldn't vouch for Tara or stand up to Xander, no one would.

"Are you alright?" the male voice said, slowing his pace. He approached like he was moving toward a wounded animal. One hand, palm out, was extended toward her. "I'm not here to hurt you. I just want to help."

Could she trust this stranger?

Did she have a choice?

2

"My name is Rowan," he said, easing toward the scared-out-of-her-wits lady, who was now curled in a ball like she was protecting her internal organs for the blow that was about to come. His first thought was that she must have escaped a domestic abuse situation, which caused his hands to fist. "Is he around? Is that why you ran?"

The woman turned her head toward him, and then blinked up at him. With the moonlight positioned just right, he caught a glimpse of the most stunning pair of violet eyes. He could also see blood on her face and arms. Was she injured?

"Help me," she managed to say, though it looked to take quite an effort through all the shivering. She had on jeans, a hoodie, and tennis shoes. Not exactly the outfit of a hiker or a camper. The denim was soaked up to her thighs.

"That's what I'm here to do," he said, extending a hand, wishing he'd brought his jacket to throw over her so she didn't freeze to death. "Can you sit up?"

The woman reached up to take his hand. Last minute,

she grabbed hold of his wrist. Using the advantage of being on the ground, she tugged his arm down and rolled, causing him to dive forward into a roll. He came up on his feet but she managed to get the better end of the stick. Or knife in this case. *His* knife.

"Come any closer and I'll stab you straight through the heart," she threatened, shifting her weight foot-to-foot while in a wide stance. She swayed side to side as she thrust the blade toward him.

"You don't want to do that," he said, realizing for the first time the blood on her arms probably didn't belong to her. Her teeth chattered so loudly, the sound echoed. "I have food and a tent. If we stay out here exposed much longer, we can kiss our toes and fingertips goodbye. Possibly the tips of our noses too."

The woman blinked, confused. "Wait. No one sent you?"

"No," he countered, just as perplexed as she looked. "Why would anyone send me? And who..."

It dawned on him that she might have escaped a women's prison. Although, he didn't remember any being out this way, not that he was suddenly an expert. Folks went to the forest for all kinds of reasons, hiding out being one of them. He was still angry—and, honestly, somewhat amused—by the fact she'd come up with his knife. Not that it mattered much in this situation, but he had a passing curiosity about why she had martial arts skills in the first place.

Was there some trauma in the past? His mind circled back to her escaping an abusive relationship.

"I don't know who did this to you," he said, shivering, "but I'm freezing so if you'll politely hand my knife over, I'll get out of your hair."

"This might come in handy," she said. "Why would I give it back to you?"

He locked gazes with those violet babies. "Because it belongs to me and I'm heading back to my warm tent."

"You'll do that?" she asked, still swaying and shivering. "You'll walk away and forget you ever saw me?"

"Do I want to know why you're out here alone?" he asked point blank.

"Oh, I'm not alone," she warned, but there was no conviction in her voice.

Rowan put his hands up, palms out, in the surrender position. "I'm sorry for whatever you're going through. I'd like to help. In all honestly, I'm offering food and warmth for a night until you get your bearings in the morning. But I also intend to stay alive in the process. So, you can either accept my help, hand back my knife, and follow me to my camp, or you can become a human Popsicle out here all by your lonesome. The choice is yours."

Rather than stand around and try to cajole her any longer, which would have been fruitless anyway, he turned back toward camp and took a couple of steps. A few seconds later, he heard the whir of a knife as it passed by his ear, missing by less than a foot, and stuck in the tree two feet ahead and to his right.

Rowan cracked a smile. He couldn't help himself. When he turned around to speak, the mystery woman was gone and he was left wondering how she disappeared without a sound.

Rather than look a gift horse in the mouth, he grabbed the handle of his knife and yanked until the tree trunk released the blade. There were so many questions about the brunette surfacing as he made the trek back to his camp. What was she doing out here? Why was there blood on her forearm? She'd been wearing nothing more than jeans and a sweater along with tennis shoes, the shoes an unusual choice for this terrain. She wasn't dressed for the cold, which gave him the impression she'd ended up here instead of planning a trip. The blood could be human or animal. It could have been hers too. He couldn't get a good enough look at her to figure it out.

Given the weather, he assumed she escaped to the forest, where she believed she could hide out. She'd also asked if anyone had sent him, as though he might be working for someone. Had she gotten herself involved in some type of criminal organization? Was she in the witness protection program? On the run?

The very real fear in her eyes had him circling back to her running away from someone or possibly a group.

No matter what the circumstances, he was still half-amused, half-reeling from the fact she'd gotten the drop on him. Rowan guessed there was a first for everything. Growing up on the family cattle ranch with all those siblings and cousins had made him a decent fighter. They'd chased each other into the woods, hidden from each other, and generally pushed each other's buttons growing up. All of which was probably the reason they were all good at tracking down poachers. Those were known quantities. Types of folks he was very well acquainted with. The mystery woman was different. Special?

Rowan had underestimated the lady in the forest once. He wouldn't make the same mistake again. Which was the reason he didn't call her out for the fact she was currently following him. If she wouldn't freeze to death or otherwise need the help, he would lead her away from his camp. Since he didn't have the heart to leave her to her own devices, he let her do her thing on her terms. She had to know that she wouldn't make it through the next hour without developing hypothermia after jumping into the creek, which also made no sense. With the freezing cold temperatures, why would she willingly go into the water?

The mystery woman either fell in by accident or wasn't thinking rationally. She seemed lucid when he'd spoken to her, though. She had the presence of mind to trick him. He shook his head and cracked a smile.

He'd fallen for the helpless victim routine. That had to be one of the oldest tricks in the book. *Damn.*

Back at the campsite, he grabbed his jacket and then built a fire in a matter of minutes. The mystery woman might be waiting for him to go to sleep before showing herself. Would she raid his supplies? Try to stab him with his own knife after he dozed off?

"Come on out," he said as he warmed his hands above the campfire.

She didn't.

He didn't believe for a second that she hadn't followed him. The occasional twig snap had clued him in even though she'd been stealth otherwise.

"I'm serious," he said. "I'm not going to hurt you."

Nothing.

"Your stubborn streak might just kill you," he finally said on a sharp sigh, facing the opposite direction of where she hid so he wouldn't scare her off completely.

The female emerged from the trees to his left, exactly where he thought she was. Good to know he hadn't lost all his skills.

"You said you have food," she said, making a beeline to the fire. Her teeth chattered so loudly he was surprised the noise hadn't given her away before.

He immediately stood up and retrieved his sleeping bag. "Take off those wet clothes."

"Excuse me?" she said defensively, folding her arms across her chest like she could somehow block him out with the move.

"You're risking hypothermia at this point," he explained calmly. "Don't worry, I won't look and even if I did, you don't have anything I haven't seen before anyway."

Rowan turned his back to her and held out his arm with the sleeping bag draped over it. He wasn't trying to be a jerk, but they needed to act fast because he wasn't kidding about the hypothermia part. Not only would his trip end up cut short, but he would most likely have to carry her over his shoulder to safety. It would be a long hike down in the cold, made worse by the weight he'd be carrying. No thanks. If he could warm her up, maybe convince her to stay for the night, he could give her directions on navigating down the mountain in the morning when the sun came up and the storm past.

The last part of his comment must have set her off because he heard her strip off her clothing while issuing a disgusted grunt. A few seconds later, she grabbed the sleeping bag off his arm. Then came, "You can turn around now."

He did, and got hit with another jolt of attraction with her standing this close. His physical reaction was inappropriate under the circumstances, not to mention unwelcomed. "Better?"

"Much," she said through chattering teeth. The bag was wrapped around her. She moved as close to the fire as she could without sitting in it.

"I'm Rowan Firebrand, by the way," he said as he retrieved a food pouch.

She nodded but didn't offer her name. There wasn't a hint of recognition in her eyes either, which was a welcomed relief. Fewer folks out here knew who a Firebrand was. The family's reputation didn't follow him like a dark cloud hovering overhead, waiting to rain down on him.

"You can make up a name if you don't want to tell me the real one," he said before holding up a finger to indicate he'd be right back. He collected water from the creek in the tin cup and then returned to the site. Her lips were no longer purple, which was a good sign she was warming up. "Did you decide?"

"Tara," she said, huddled over as she warmed up.

"Real or fake?" he asked.

"Does it matter?" she asked, looking up. When their gazes met, an unfamiliar jolt blasted from inside the center of his chest. What the hell was that about? It felt a whole lot like attraction, the intensity of which he'd never experienced before.

Rowan dismissed it. He was clearly losing it from lack of sleep.

"I guess not," he said as he hooked the metal rod into the tin cup just like he'd done before. "I hope you like chicken and broccoli with rice casserole."

"Are you kidding?" she asked, incredulous. "Because I'd kill for a meal right now." Her expression morphed like she regretted those words, causing more questions to surface that he didn't have answers to.

"Give me a few minutes," he said. "And you don't have to kill anything."

THIS MAN WAS ALMOST TOO good to be true.

"Real," she said, figuring she owed him at least that much, since he'd been nothing but kind. It was the reason she'd returned his knife rather than keep the only protection she'd found so far, well, other than the sharp rock she kept in her back pocket. It had saved her life but was also how she'd killed Xander. A murder weapon wasn't exactly a lucky charm and yet she hadn't been able to get rid of the one thing that had provided a sense of security until now. "And thank you."

"You're welcome," he said, bringing the water inside the cup to a boil. He poured the water into a pouch then produced a fork, which he used to stir. When he decided it was done, he handed over the pouch along with a fork. "I thought your stomach could use something calm like, chicken and rice."

Tara took the offering and immediately dug in. The pouch was empty in a matter of minutes, the food was surprisingly good, and she was finally warm. After not believing she would make it out of this situation alive, she was beginning to see a glimmer of hope.

Was it naïve to think she could leave this forest and start over in a new city? Could she leave the only family she'd ever known, in order to save her own life? Tara shook her head as a tear escaped. She had to find a way to change her identity and visit her mother, because she couldn't be relocated without it causing a stir. Tara couldn't do that to Grace, the only mother she'd ever known. Not to the woman who'd taken Tara in despite her background, loved her, and given her the first and only home she'd ever known. She couldn't do that to Grace Goodman, not when Grace needed Tara the most.

"Once again, thank you for the food," she said to Rowan. The term 'easy on the eyes' came to mind when it came to the handsome stranger. His eyes were sea-blue, his jaw honest and squared, his lips thick, and his sandy-blond hair cut tight to what looked like a perfectly-shaped head. Very few could pull off bald, but it would look good on this man. Then again, there probably wasn't much that wouldn't. His physical size had scared her at first. He was tall and muscled.

Strong enough to protect her?

There was no way she was pulling him into her nightmare. He didn't deserve it. No one did.

Rowan took the empty pouch from her and disappeared. She'd overhead campers packing up because of bear sightings in the area, and figured he was disposing of the trash in a manner that wouldn't attract predators. There were other deadly beasts out here besides bears. Mountain lions killed more folks than bears anyway. She involuntarily shivered at the thought. Another darker thought struck. Humans were apex predators, killing more often than the others combined. What did that say about humanity? What did that say about her?

The handsome stranger finagled a few branches near the fire, creating a warming rack where he placed her clothing. She got up to help but he stopped her with a hand.

"I got this," he said. "You've been through a lot. You should rest and stay warm."

Could she? Was it even possible she could grab an hour or two of shuteye while her clothing dried? Sneak away long before sunrise?

Why did she feel a sudden and deep sense of loss at the thought of leaving a stranger?

Probably because it was the first time in a very long time someone made her feel safe.

"Am I allowed to ask what you're doing out here?" he

asked. His deep timbre washing over her and through her, warming her from the inside out just like the campfire.

"I'd rather not say," she admitted.

"Okay," he said. "That's fair. Thanks for your honesty."

"What about you?" she asked, turning the tables.

"I came here to get away from home for a while and clear my head," he said, rubbing his hands together over the fire. "Home is Texas, by the way."

"Wife troubles?" she asked, realizing she hadn't checked for a wedding ring, not that everyone wore them.

"No wife," he said.

"Kids?" she asked.

"None of those either," he answered. "You?"

She shook her head. Knowing the two of them were single shouldn't have a physical effect on her. It shouldn't make her heart leap. They were strangers and this was an impossible situation. Not to mention the fact she would never be able to trust anyone ever again after Xander. And the other fact she would be spending the rest of her life behind bars after what she'd done.

This man was different and he deserved better. She squared up with him from across the fire. "You have questions."

"Yes, I do," he admitted.

"I can't answer any of them," she said, figuring this was the point where he would kick her out of his camp. "Are you okay with that?"

"What if I'm not?" he asked.

"Then I should go right now," she said, making a move to get up, hoping he'd stop her. Her heart sank to her stomach when he didn't.

3

Rowan hesitated with his answer in order to feel Tara out on how serious she was about leaving. Apparently, she was dead serious if his questions needed answers. "Stay. We'll figure it out."

"I'm trouble," Tara said. He noticed that she didn't say she was *in* trouble but that she *is* trouble. He noted the subtle but powerful difference.

"What if I like trouble?" he asked with half a smile.

"This is serious," she said with a look.

This was probably a long shot but he had to ask. "Any chance law enforcement can help?"

Her face washed of all color at the mention of the law. It was abundantly clear that law enforcement wasn't an option.

"You've done enough for me already," she began, twisting her fingers together. "I'll only drag you down."

"You couldn't," he said.

Her eyebrow shot up. "You have no idea what you're up against."

How would she navigate her way to safety anyway? "Do you have a cell phone?"

She shook her head.

"Don't have or don't own?" he asked. Those were two very different questions.

"It's not on me," she admitted.

"Lost?" he asked.

"That's enough questions," she said with a cautionary glance.

"Stay the night?" he asked, wishing he could find a way to ease her concerns. From across the fire, he could see her pulse pound at the base of her throat. Continuing the discussion would only have one result. She would bolt and that would put her in danger.

"I said no more questions."

"It was a request," he pointed out.

"I should probably go," she said but there was no conviction in those words.

"The storm will shut down any searches for the rest of tonight, in case that's what you're worried about," he said with the hope he could reason some sense into the situation. She'd been through some kind of ordeal that she wasn't ready to discuss. His mind snapped to her being in an abusive relationship and having to fight her way out as making the most sense, but he had no idea if that was true. She was strong and knew how to defend herself. Still. She could have gotten into a fight with her boyfriend while out camping. It might have ended physically, which would explain the blood. An animal attack didn't make sense because it wouldn't be something to hide, so he ruled out bears and the like. The fact she had no supplies, no cell, and no idea where she was or where she was going made him circle back to the fight hypothesis.

He studied her as she decided her next move.

"I hiked a couple of hours to get to this spot," he said. "Continue on down that path and you'll eventually end up in a parking lot if you don't end up too far off course." He didn't feel the need to point out the fact snow was piling up.

"It's not getting any warmer out here tonight," she reasoned, glancing around. "As far as I know, no one knows to look for me."

The last statement was interesting, but he wasn't about to touch it when she was so close to agreeing to stick around. He was serious about not being able to sleep if she was out there wandering around in the freezing cold. He could try to give her exact directions as to how to get back to where he started, but cell service was asking for a lot out here. He'd headed this way for its remote landscape and lack of connectivity. Plus, finding the path while it was snowing wasn't exactly ideal conditions and she didn't exactly have a vehicle waiting for her down there as far as he could tell. Asking if she was from around here might spook her off, so he ditched the idea of trying to find out how familiar she might be with the area.

Tara cocked her head to one side. "Where would I sleep?"

"In the tent with me," he said. "We can share the sleeping bag. Our body heat will help keep us warm."

Tara's gaze shifted to the small tent. She seemed to be calculating the odds of survival if she struck out on her own and decided not to take him up on his offer. She didn't strike him as foolish or reckless despite the circumstances. "Okay. Thank you."

"Good," he said, a little surprised she agreed. "I've had a long travel day and I'm beyond tired. The storm is kicking back up, so I'd very much like to put this fire out and hit the sack."

Her gaze dropped to where she clasped the sleeping bag tight in her hand. Right. She wasn't wearing anything underneath.

He stood up to check on her clothes. "Your undergarments are dry but not the rest. I don't want to risk leaving the fire going, so we'll have to leave the wet clothes out overnight and start the fire again in the morning. Okay?"

She nodded.

"Alright then," he said. "I have an extra flannel shirt that should be long enough to double as pajamas for you."

Her face brightened. "That would be nice."

"Hold on."

He retrieved his favorite blue flannel from his rucksack inside the tent before handing it over. Tara turned her back to him after taking the offering. She slipped into it without losing the sleeping bag that she currently used as a blanket. He checked her socks.

"These are dry," he said, handing them over next. "Those should help hold heat in." Most heat was lost through the feet and head.

She slipped her socks on next and he was pretty sure he heard a mewl of pleasure. "Those are warm."

Exhaustion was setting in. Rowan knew sleeping body-to-body with the beautiful stranger would have an effect on him, but he couldn't imagine anyone or anything keeping him from passing out once he climbed inside the tent.

"Ready?" Tara asked. He wasn't touching that question with a ten-foot pole. Instead, he shook his head and put the fire out.

"Your clothes should keep here for the night," he said as he led her into the tent. He toed off his boots and set them

Rowan: Firebrand Cowboys 25

next to the rucksack like before. "We'll have to use the sleeping bag as a mattress. It's too small to wrap around both of us."

"Not if we get really close," Tara said as she slipped in beside him after he laid out the bag. "Here. Try this. We might not be able to zip it up but we'll get some coverage for both of us."

She tugged him closer until their bodies were flush, arms and legs entwined. "Is this okay?"

"Better," he said, hearing the huskiness in his own voice. "This will keep us warm for the night."

Tara settled into the crook of his arm. He felt her heart battering the inside of her ribcage. But it didn't take long for her steady, even breathing to tell him she was asleep. He wasn't sure why he waited, or how he managed to keep his eyes open considering how tired he'd been. Knowing she could sleep—the ultimate act of trust in this situation—gave him a sense of pride. He wanted her to trust him. It was the only way he could help her even though she'd made it clear she didn't want anyone involved.

How bad could her situation be?

Because he'd picked up on the fact that she was trying to protect him by keeping him out of her business. She wouldn't do that if she was a bad human being. No. Tara got herself tangled up in something over her head. And he had tomorrow morning to figure out how to convince her to let him help, since his idea of going to the law had been shut down.

And why was that?

Did she believe the law wouldn't be on her side? There were battered women's shelters that would step in with resources to help. He didn't know much about them, but he'd heard there were good ones out there. They could find one together if needed. The question of whether or not she would leave wasn't one he could answer at present, and she was being tightlipped about her situation. Did she think her boyfriend or ex-boyfriend, whatever the case may be, would come after Rowan for helping?

Let him try.

Rowan had never stepped away from a challenge and had no intention of doing it now. At this point, however, he was putting the cart before the horse. This was all just one big guessing game. There were other possibilities—possibilities that didn't jive with Tara being the decent person he believed her to be.

Again, she probably wouldn't have returned his knife if she was truly bad.

As he started to drift off, she mumbled something unintelligible. Still, it kept him from falling asleep.

"Leave me alone."

Those words were clear as day. Tara wriggled her body, something that didn't help his libido, as she seemed unsettled. Was it a fight with her boyfriend?

"Stop."

If this escalated, he'd go ahead and wake her. Right now, he didn't have the heart since she'd looked every bit as exhausted as he felt.

"Xan..."

She mumbled the last word so this was all he could make out. Xan? What on earth could that mean? Xanax? Was she taking some kind of anti-depressant? Was she off her meds? He'd heard those were serious and had to be weaned off of. Had someone taken her meds from her?

His mind was spinning into a direction that didn't feel right.

Thankfully, she settled down and sank into him.

No, it didn't help his libido but he wasn't a hormonal teenager who couldn't keep his hands to himself or control his instincts.

Instead, he closed his eyes and gave into sleep.

Tara wasn't sure how long she'd slept the previous night, but it was the first good night she'd had in longer than she cared to count. Could she slip out from the sleeping bag without disturbing the generous man who'd done nothing but help her?

A growing part of her didn't want to leave this spot. Ever. This was also the first time she'd felt safe in far too long and she wasn't in a rush to jump back into reality—a reality that meant she needed to leave right now.

Living in Denver, she never really came up to the mountains. Certainly not to ski. There were too many reports of skiers flying off the mountain to their deaths, for her to take up the sport. She had, however, been secretly taking self-defense classes. First, online. Then, she'd managed to leave the visits with her mom half an hour early to meet with a trainer. She insisted on paying in cash, a move the trainer didn't mind. He let her in the backdoor while Xander was on shift with Denver PD.

Tara was still trying to figure out how she'd ended up entwined with that monster, although his brother was by far the greater of two evils. In the beginning, Xander had been charming. He'd stopped by to see her while she sat beside her mother's bed, having been the responding officer to her mom's car crash. He'd shown his good side, only his good side.

And, to be honest, Tara had never felt so alone while

sitting in that hospital, waiting to find out if her beloved mom was going to live or die. And then again when she'd had to be the one who had to make the call as to taking her mom off the breathing machine to see if she could breathe on her own.

Looking back, there'd been signs about Xander. His quick temper with others should have warned her away, but she'd made excuses for him because he had such a good side. He'd gone out of his way to make sure her mom ended up in the best possible rehab facility, a fact he'd reminded her of time and time again when things became bad between them. Their whirlwind courtship should have raised red flags too. He'd said he loved her within weeks of dating. She didn't see his possessive side until after she'd moved in with him. And even then, it had started with jealousy that she thought was kind of cute.

The first time, it was one of the 'hire a college boy' movers that Xander said looked at her too much. He'd said she shouldn't be flirty with the twenty-year-old. To be honest, she thought Xander was being playful. She didn't take his moodiness seriously. All it had taken to get back on course was to remind him that he was the only guy for her. They'd had the best makeup sex as a result.

The reassurances that he was her number one had to come more and more frequently. The next time, it was the grocery stocker who kept staring at her backside, according to Xander. He moved himself in between her and the gawker, or so he'd called him. The guy was just trying to be friendly and do his job. But Xander didn't see it that way, so she started shopping while he was at work.

Then, there were hosts at restaurants or waiters that were suspect. It was unreasonable to think every guy in her vicinity was trying to hit on her. She'd had to repeat those words until they'd become a mantra. The other one was that he was the only one she wanted to be with.

Tara knew Xander's work was stressful. She blamed his short fuse on work stress but she'd never felt more trapped in a relationship. His actions escalated so slowly, like bringing a pot to boil on low heat, that it didn't register at the time. Not until their lives were entwined to the point it would take time to untangle them did she realize she had to get out.

When she'd sat him down and tried to talk to him about their relationship, he blew up.

By the end, he'd tried to convince her that she was imagining things and that all was good between them. She got the message loud and clear, though. Leave and she would regret it. And then his brother paid her a visit. He'd threatened her to within an inch of her life if she left his younger brother. Said law enforcement looked out for each other and didn't take kindly to traitors. He'd told her that if she left Xander, she would pay a steep price. And then, he'd dropped a picture of her mom on the coffee table before walking out. Apparently, no one left a Smythe.

At that point, she realized this was far more serious than she feared and leaving was going to require a whole lot of finesse. Because there was no way she could leave her mom, and Tara didn't have an endless bank account that would allow her to move her mom to a new facility and change both of their identities in the process.

Now?

Xander was dead. She killed him. And she was in even deeper with no way out. His brother would hunt her down and make her pay if it was the last thing he did.

The only saving grace in this entire situation was the staff at Safe Rehab. Several had witnessed the way Xander treated her and pulled her aside on different occasions to ask if she was alright or needed a place to stay. They'd promised to take care of her mom when she couldn't be there.

Could they watch twenty-four-seven?

Xander's brother T.J. wouldn't hurt Tara's mother. Would he? What would be the point?

To punish her, a little voice in the back of her mind pointed out. What could he possibly gain other than revenge? Especially when doing so would make it easier for her to go into hiding. Her mom was the only reason she wouldn't leave town. He had to know it.

Not being able to call and check in was the worst feeling. Her cell was lost. It had gone over the side of the mountain when Xander found her trying to run away.

The thought Xander would be given a hero's funeral while she would be blamed, hunted, and then jailed for the rest of her life sat sick in her stomach.

Tara looked at Rowan. She couldn't get the decent and honest human sleeping beside her involved in the shitshow that had become her life. There was no way she could do that to a good person. He didn't deserve to become embroiled in this mess.

Could she slip out of the tent, locate her clothes, and then take off without disturbing him?

The wind had stopped howling and the sun was out. That had to be a good sign. Right?

As slowly and quietly as she could manage, she untangled her body from his. The cover was more of a challenge because she was completely wrapped inside the sleeping bag. The open side, the zipper part was on the other side of Rowan.

Before she could so much as flinch, Tara was flipped on

her back and a blade was to her throat. She stared into wild eyes—eyes that blinked a couple of times before recognition dawned.

"Oh hell, I'm sorry," Rowan said but she couldn't speak and she couldn't stop shaking.

4

Rowan eased off, hating the fact he stared into fearful eyes. "I track poachers back at the ranch and that was instinct."

He barely finished speaking as Tara scrambled to unzip and leave the tent. She couldn't get out of there fast enough.

"Hey," he said, following her. He didn't like what had just gone down and needed to apologize again. The woman had already been traumatized by someone, a male if he was reading the situation correctly. The last thing he wanted to do was make it worse on her or give her the impression all men were jerks.

She grabbed her stiff, cold garments off the makeshift rack.

"Those aren't dry or warm," he said. "Give me fifteen minutes and you can be on your way."

"I can't believe I let that happen," she muttered under her breath along with a few other choice words. "You were on top of me so fast and I couldn't defend myself."

"No offense, but I'm damn good," he said a little more defensively than intended.

Rowan: Firebrand Cowboys 33

She whirled around on him.

"That shouldn't have gone down like that," she defended, heated. Her cheeks were flush and he could see her breath, which was coming out in bursts of frustration. "I've been training for months now. No one, not even you, should be able to catch me off guard or trip me up like you just did in there." She pointed to the tent as an angry tear rolled down her cheek. She sniffed once and wiped it away.

At first, he'd believed she was mad at him. Now, he realized she was mad at herself.

"It wasn't your fault," he insisted. "I caught you off guard."

"Yeah?" she said. "Being caught off guard could get me killed."

He stared at her for a long moment. "Who is after you and why?"

"I already told you the subject is off limits," she said as she tried to slip a leg into frozen jeans. It was impossible and all her frustration bubbled up until he thought her head might explode like in those old cartoons.

"Hold on." He put a hand up before taking a minute to light a fire. At least, he could give her warm clothes and breakfast before she took off. Then, it would be best if he never saw her again. She'd clearly gotten herself into a mess, and she had no intention of talking or allowing him to give her a hand beyond last night and possibly breakfast this morning. As much as he didn't want to walk away from a person in need, he'd learned the hard way that it was impossible to assist folks who didn't want to be helped. The fire came to life. He rubbed his hands together to warm them. "Alright. Give the clothes five to ten minutes and they'll be wearable. It'll give me enough time to make breakfast and coffee before sending you on your way."

Looking defeated, she fixed the clothes back on the rack and reclaimed her seat from last night. Seeing her in his flannel shirt didn't do good things to his heart but it was something he had to ignore. After breakfast, he planned to never see this complicated woman again. It was too hard on him to watch a train wreck without being able to throw her a lifeline.

Tara whatever-her-last-name-was, was complicated. He needed complicated in his life like he needed an axe in his skull. In fact, he'd left Texas and the ranch to get away from complicated.

He located his toiletry bag inside his rucksack before handing over a small, foldable toothbrush.

"You have two of these?" she asked, sounding surprised.

"Yes."

"Why?" she asked as she unfolded the blue toiletry. He squeezed a little toothpaste on the brushes before taking care of his. When he didn't answer, she continued, "It's just that you only carry basic necessities. One fork that I saw you wash out after I used it. One coffee tin that you also boil water in. I'm surprised you'd have two toothbrushes."

"You're right about me carrying necessities," he said. "Have you ever finger-brushed your teeth?"

"Yes," she admitted. "It's pretty awful."

"The spare toothbrush doesn't take up much in the way of room, considering it folds over," he said. "I consider it a necessity in case something happens to mine. I can improvise most anything else but I lost a toothbrush once out on the range. Had to go four days finger brushing my teeth. I'll never do that again."

She nodded as her gaze darted around. Her panic levels were still high. She looked like she half-expected someone to jump out from behind a tree at any moment. There wasn't much he could do about it either. Not unless she let him in, which he highly doubted was going to happen.

"If I ever meet the bastard who did this to you, he'll live to regret it," Rowan muttered under his breath. The fact she'd taken self-defense classes, in addition to everything else he'd observed since last night, caused him to draw the conclusion his first instinct had been correct. She was on the run from someone who intended to hurt her.

"He's not the one I'm worried about anymore," she said so low that he almost didn't hear her as she turned her back and walked to the creek.

Rowan joined her with the small amount of saved water from last night in one hand and his toothbrush in the other. She finished first, so he handed the tin over for her to rinse her mouth out. He used the opposite side when it was his turn.

Her last statement had more questions swirling. She wasn't worried about the boyfriend or ex. Then who?

This made even less sense. It dawned on him that she might have been dating a married man. But then why take self-defense? Granted, every person should know how to defend themselves in case of an attack. He'd had plenty of experience growing up with brothers and cousins, not to mention being chased by wild boar and stalked by a mountain lion once or twice that he knew of. He'd learned the hard way how to defend himself against almost anything, except the pain that came with knowing his mother was in jail. Knowing she deserved to be there was even worse.

Rowan realized that he hadn't been thinking about his own problems since Tara blew into his life, much like last night's storm. And she was about to leave almost as fast. He boiled water and located two food pouches. Sharing cut down on his supplies but he wasn't worried about the couple of meals he'd give to her. He could always hike back down the mountain and go to the store if he couldn't find anything to eat on the mountain, which was highly unlikely. Plus, he had a fishhook and some line. All he needed was a good stick to complete the fishing pole.

"This morning's menu is eggs, bacon, and biscuits with gravy," he said as he retrieved two pouches.

"I have no idea how they pull it off, but the food in those pouches is beyond good," she said as she squatted down beside the fire, wrapping her arms around her knees. And then came a sharp sigh. She locked gazes as he handed over a pouch along with a fork. "I know you have to have so many questions. It would be best for you if you forgot you ever saw me. In fact, if anyone comes asking, and I mean anyone, please don't mention that you saw me. I wouldn't normally ask someone to lie, but I..."

"You don't have to explain," he said as he fixed his own pouch. "I got it. You're in some kind of trouble that you've been anticipating for a while. It has to do with a man who is a boyfriend or ex. For some reason, the situation has gone south and you had to escape to the woods."

"That about sums it up," she said, but a look passed behind those violet eyes that said there was so much more to the story. "Still, it's best for you if you don't know me."

"I don't know you," he countered. "You could have given me a fake first name and I have no idea what your last name is. Problem solved."

"Yeah," she agreed but her shoulders deflated.

"Have you been alone long?" he asked.

"No," she said. "But it feels like a whole lifetime."

Rowan cleaned off the fork with an alcohol wipe before digging into his food. It wasn't exactly of the caliber of his aunt's famous meatballs, but it was as close to real eggs and bacon as he was going to get for a while. But then, that was his choice. Soon enough, he wouldn't have this much for breakfast once the pouches ran out. He could ration the rest to make the food last longer. Go ahead and fish today to save on dinner tonight.

"Can I ask why you're out here all alone?" she asked, turning the tables.

"I'm an open book," he said after chewing and swallowing a bite using the spoon he'd packed. "My mother is in jail for attempted murder, which she is guilty of, by the way. My friend wants me to move to north Texas and start a business, which would mean abandoning the family's cattle ranch."

"I'm sorry about your mother," Tara said when she could finally speak after her jaw fell slack. "I think."

He chuckled. "I couldn't have said it better myself. I'm not sure what to think about the whole situation at home."

"Sounds complicated," she said.

Exactly the reason he didn't need more complications in his life, no matter how drawn to Tara he was. "You could say that."

"What about the business idea?" she asked. "You don't want to do it?"

"It sounds great and I'd love working with my buddy," he said. "But I'm a cattle rancher. It's in my blood and all I've ever known. It's also my legacy. We inherited the cattle, ranch, and mineral rights after my grandfather passed away."

"Doesn't sound that complex to me," she said.

"I gave you the abridged version," he responded.

"There's your answer then," she said with a smile that didn't reach her eyes.

"It's a little more involved than that," he said.

"How so?"

"I come from a big family who also works the ranch," he said. "We've been split for so long that even trying to mend fences seems like a temporary fix." He shrugged. "I guess I got tired of all the infighting when we should be getting along, working together."

"Does your mother being in jail have anything to do with the reason for the fighting?" she asked, cocking an eyebrow. She leaned closer to him and tilted her head.

"You could say that," he said with a chuckle. It wasn't funny, but the situation was so out there it was almost impossible to believe. There wasn't much else to do but laugh at this point.

"I've always wanted to belong to a big family," she said, staring off into the trees. "I didn't realize how hard it might be to get along with so many conflicting personalities. Of course, there would be disagreements."

"We're all strong-minded, so that doesn't help," he said. "Our grandfather, the Marshall, pitted my father against my uncle until we buried the old man. I guess we've all been left to clean up the mess."

"Do you love your family?" she asked, surprising him.

"Without question," he said. "But it's not that easy. Big families have a lot of moving parts. In my experience, most of those parts are trying to move in all different directions."

She laughed before bringing her hand up to cover her mouth and stifle it. "Sorry. I just had a cartoon image of everyone in a rowboat trying to paddle in different directions."

"Don't be," he said. "If we didn't develop a sense of humor about life, we'd lose our minds. Right?"

"Yes to that," she said emphatically. "Sounds like yours is

the kind of family that might be worth fighting for. Difficult as they may be."

"There's a point when it gets to be too much and I happen to think life should be easier than this," he admitted. Rowan wasn't much of a talker but opening up to Tara was easier. It was probably just easier to talk to a stranger than someone he knew, someone close to him and the situation back home.

"I keep asking myself all the time when life got so messy," she admitted. "And I couldn't agree more that it should be simpler. But life has a mind of its own."

"That's the truth," he agreed. They both smiled. Real, genuine smiles. The kind that made two people feel connected when they looked into each other's eyes. Neither broke contact right away and it felt like one of the most intimate moments in recent memory.

"I'm sorry about what you're going through," she said, holding his gaze with those violet eyes of hers.

He just looked at her. "I'm here by choice, to clear my head. I can't imagine running away *to* here, especially when you're not prepared. You could easily have frozen to death last night."

"Might have made it easier," she said on an exhale that caused her shoulders to deflate.

And didn't that cause a whole bunch of questions to form inside Rowan's head.

∼

"I APOLOGIZE for trying to sneak away this morning without saying goodbye," Tara said to the handsome stranger. Although, oddly enough, he didn't feel like a stranger any longer. Plus, she knew his name. Rowan Firebrand. The last name was vaguely familiar but she couldn't figure out why. Might just be the circumstances causing her to want something to hold onto. "You've done so much for me already. I didn't want you to feel responsible for doing anything else."

"I wouldn't have felt—"

She threw a hand up to stop him midsentence. It worked.

"It's the way you're made," she countered. "I'm guessing there's some kind of rancher code, or maybe you've served in the Marines at one point, since you seem unwilling to leave anyone behind."

He shook his head at the last bit.

"Rancher's honor, then," she settled on.

"We take care of each other," he explained. "It goes way back to our roots before everything could be delivered by tapping a phone screen and we had to rely on one another to survive. It's in our DNA at this point."

"It's honorable," she said, feeling the heat crawl up her neck at the compliment. "More people should be like you." She meant those words with everything inside her. How wonderful would the world be if there were more folks like Rowan and less like Xander and his brother?

"Watch out there," he said with a warning look that made her sit up straighter. "Pretty soon I'll take that as a compliment and think you might actually not want to strangle me when I go to sleep."

Tara laughed. She couldn't help herself. "As I remember, you were the one with the knife to my throat after I flinched."

"Sorry about that," he said. "Job hazard, I'm afraid. And too many nights without female companionship."

Now it was his turn to blush. Of course, she didn't believe a word of it. Someone as gorgeous as Rowan would have a long line of women ready to spend time with them. But he didn't strike her as the playboy type, despite his ridiculous good looks and charm. No. He was a one-woman man if he decided to let anyone in, which she doubted. The fact he was out here alone to solve his problems told her all she needed to know about how high his walls were.

"It wasn't personal," she conceded, bringing her hand up to rub her neck at the spot the blade had touched. One wrong move and the outcome might have been very different. She swallowed hard. "No harm done." Then, she caught his gaze. "But it seems like you have a past too."

"I already told you about the poachers," he explained.

"I wasn't talking about the knife," she said.

"Oh," he said with a confused look on his face.

"There's a reason you came out here by yourself to work out your problems," she said, wondering if she should call him out.

"It's how I think best," he said with a cocked eyebrow.

"Alone," she clarified.

"They are *my* problems," he said.

"You have a big family," she continued. "Is there no one you trust?"

Rowan didn't immediately answer.

"What are you going to do?" she pressed.

"That's what I'm here to figure out," he countered. "I need to clear my head so I can think straight again."

"Because of your mother?"

"Yes," he said "Among other things."

"Do you want to talk about it?" she asked, then put a hand up. "Before we say anything else, we're not likely ever going to see each other again after this morning. And, sometimes, it's easier to open up to someone you know you're never going to be in the same room with. The only thing we definitively know about each other is our first names. Well, and your last."

"Your name is really Tara?" he asked, sounding surprised.

"I said it is," she admitted. "I'd rather not speak at all than lie."

Rowan nodded as he leaned forward, resting his elbow on his thighs and clasping his hands together. "There was someone in my life once. Someone I believed was special."

5

Rowan never expected to open up to anyone about what had happened with Alicia, but Tara was right. They were never going to see each other again and he liked talking to her. What was the harm?

"What happened?" Tara asked, leaning in as she rubbed her hands warm near the fire.

"I already told you about my family and how much work they can be," he continued. "On top of everything else, they're nosy when it comes to each other's business." He paused. "Well, that's not exactly fair. Not everyone. But word spreads fast, so I decided not to introduce Alicia to anyone until I was ready."

"Alicia was the someone special I take it," she clarified.

"That's right," he said. "She knew where I stood on ever having kids."

"Which is?"

"I don't ever want to put another human being through the hell I've been through growing up a Firebrand," he said flat out.

She nodded and something dawned behind her eyes. Recognition of his family name?

"Anyway," he continued before she could piece it all together. "I was upfront with Alicia about never wanting kids and she was supposedly fine with it. She'd had a messed up childhood too, being bounced from parent to parent after a divorce. Both her and her sister learned to stick together in order to survive the battles over every detail of their lives, so I thought she understood where I was coming from."

"She agreed to no kids, so I don't see the problem," Tara said. "Unless she changed her mind at some point."

"I knew going in that it was a possibility," he said. "As we get older, priorities shift."

"That's true," she said. "But still. An agreement is an agreement."

"Kids were pretty much a deal breaker to me," he admitted, checking to see her reaction. "I knew where I stood, so I'd taken care of it a long time ago."

"Meaning?"

"I can't have an 'oops' baby," he explained. "In fact, I can't have children at all. Not without a medical miracle."

"Your childhood must have damaged you quite a bit to make that conscious choice and follow through with it at such a young age," she said.

"It took some convincing on my part with the doctor who agreed with you," he said. "I never mentioned the surgery to Alicia. Which was definitely my fault. But I was clear about not having kids. I was also clear about knowing that wasn't going to change. Alicia said it didn't matter to her. The two of us were all the family she needed, so I guess it didn't register as important. I knew we would have to have a sit-down at some point. I was preparing to do just that."

"And then she changed her mind?" Tara's face twisted in confusion.

"Then, she betrayed me," he said, clenching his back teeth at the memory, at the hurt she'd caused.

"Cheated?"

"Worse," he said. "She turned up pregnant and said she must have forgotten to take her birth control pills."

"Which you knew was a lie," she said, shaking her head. "That's terrible."

"And a way to trap me into marriage," he said. "Apparently, I wasn't getting there fast enough for her either."

"Damn," she said. "You knew the truth."

"There was no possible way the baby could be mine," he said. "She swore that she never cheated and that she went to a sperm bank. But I wasn't born yesterday. When I asked for proof of her visit, like an invoice or receipt, she took off. Her social media account is disabled and her cell doesn't work any longer."

"She's embarrassed?" she asked.

"And I'm left with the lingering question as to whether she cheated or if the kid could actually be mine after all," he said.

"Wouldn't that be impossible?"

"Believe me when I say that I researched the hell out of it," he said. "Turns out, it's possible, even if it's not probable."

"And now you want to confront her and, maybe, get a DNA test to make sure," she said with a look of compassion.

He blinked. "How do I move forward with anything else in my life without the answer to that question?"

"You make a good point," she said. "Do you know where she works?"

"She's on leave and her friends won't tell me where she went," he said.

"You know her best," she said. "Can you guess?"

"That's the strangest part—"

A twig broke to their left. Rowan was up with a hand extended toward her, asking her to hold on a sec in the space of a heartbeat. He circled back behind the tent and around to catch whoever or whatever was over there off guard.

A deer. It was a deer.

Rowan released the breath he'd been holding as he approached. The animal immediately checked behind, saw Rowan, and bolted.

Back at camp two minutes later, Tara leaned against a tree.

"He was a baby," she said.

"You saw him?" he asked, surprised he hadn't heard so much as a noise from her.

"I came around the other side," she admitted before tossing the knife next to the tent.

"You're fast," Rowan said. He had to give it to her.

"When your life depends on it..."

"You have no reason to trust me, but I'm a good listener," he pointed out. The danger was real for Tara. He could see it in her actions and in her eyes.

"You're a fixer," she said. "I tell you what's going on with me and you're going to try to make it right."

"We won't know if you don't try me," he said. It was a 'hail Mary' statement because there was almost zero chance she was going to discuss her situation with him.

"Plus, you were just about to tell me the strangest part," she said, redirecting the conversation. "Remember?"

He reclaimed his seat near the fire since he didn't have on enough clothes to stay warm if he got too far away from it. "Right. As I was saying. How well could I have really known someone who would deceive me to that degree? This is a major life decision we're talking about. It's not like she lied about having a job or quitting a job. Those can be big decisions too, but nothing compared to trying to make someone a father, who'd flat out said no and was honest about it from the beginning."

"You make a good point," she said.

"Plus, I should know the answer as to where she would go, and I don't," he admitted.

"Funny how we think we know someone and then they pull a major about-face on us, right?" she asked with a look of comradery. There was so much honesty and feeling in those words, he knew he'd hit the nail on the head about her running from someone who'd been important in her life.

He nodded. "I've spent a fair amount of time beating myself up for that one.".

She twisted her fingers together like she did when she was nervous. "Same here. And I've...it's easy to get down on yourself for not having better judgment when it comes to the opposite sex. It's downright shocking how different they can turn out to be. All you're left wondering is...how could I have not seen it coming?"

"We see the best in people," he surmised. "Because we see a reflection of our own personalities. Plus, I've come to realize that some folks are really good at providing a reflection of our values. We think we know them until they show their true colors, which takes time."

"Colors they hide until they've got you hooked," she said. Now, he was certain he was on the right track with her. Only, this had more to it than lying about paternity.

"It's a shame," he agreed.

Tara looked up at him and locked gazes. "Did you get reliable confirmation she's actually pregnant?"

He shrugged. "I saw a diagnosis from her doctor."

"Did you speak to her obstetrician personally?" she asked.

"No," he said. "Alicia blew up when I told her that the baby couldn't be mine. Said she could never trust me, since I withheld the information from her in the first place." He shook his head. "She turned the argument around to somehow be my fault."

"It was probably the best way for her to make herself come out as sympathetic in the situation," she added.

"She did a good job of catching me off guard." He'd been shocked.

"Had you asked her to marry you?" she asked.

"No," he said. "And I wouldn't have without having a sit-down about the vasectomy."

Tara sat quietly for a long moment.

"Surgery is an extreme measure for a young person," she said.

"So was my childhood," he countered. "It left me never wanting to have a family of my own."

"Can I ask why?" she asked. "There are plenty of people who have bad childhoods who vow to do better with the next generation rather than swear off children altogether."

Rowan nodded. "You can change your parenting style but you can't alter your DNA."

∽

As much as Tara wanted to point out how good of a person Rowan was and that his DNA would most likely be filled with that same goodness, looking at him now, she realized he wasn't ready to listen. "That's true."

"What about you?" he asked, turning the tables.

"I thought I wanted children at one time," she admitted. "Not anymore."

He leaned forward, smiled in a way that lit a campfire inside her, and lowered his voice when he said, "I mean, what are you going to do next?"

"I don't have an answer," she said, feeling a red blush crawl up her neck to her cheeks.

"Don't have one or don't want to tell me?"

"I have no clue what my next steps might be," she said on an exhale. "I didn't think that far ahead. I just bolted after everything went down..." She flashed eyes at him, a warning not to ask questions. "And didn't look back."

"You had blood on your arms last night," he pointed out. "It's why you were in the creek."

Tara got up and started pacing as fear mounted inside her. The truth of the matter was that she didn't have any idea how she was going to survive the wrath of the man who would have been her brother-in-law. T.J. was connected to the Lieutenant, who had his hands deep into Denver PD. The Lieutenant was the one calling the shots, and was the person who'd asked Xander for the 'favor' that got them into this mess.

Another twig snapped not twenty-five feet away. Tara slipped behind a tree and out of sight. The noise came from the direction of the creek. It made sense when she really thought about it. It was morning. Creatures would be searching for a water source. At least, she hoped it was an animal this time. Either way, her pulse jacked up and it was hard to breathe.

Slowly, methodically, she moved closer to the water to

get a better look. It was a raccoon in search of food. Of course, it was. She exhaled a slow breath. Sticking around was a bad idea.

Returning to camp, Rowan was nowhere to be found. Had he gone to check out the noise? It made sense he would. Calling for him would draw attention to the campsite, which was not a good idea. The noise at the creek might have been a raccoon but there could be other predators nearby.

This seemed like a good time to finish up so she could head out.

"Where do you plan to go next?" Rowan's deep timbre from behind her stirred an ache inside her chest she couldn't afford.

"I seriously have no idea," she said, turning to face him and taking a hit in the center of her chest the second she did. His spicy-campfire scent was all over her after sleeping in close quarters. Someone could get rich turning that scent into aftershave. "It's not safe to stay in one place, though. And it's not safe for you to be near me." She was panicked at the thought she'd over-shared and given herself away.

"I'm not going to tell anyone that I saw you," he reassured. She'd always been told she wore her emotions on her sleeve. "Or do anything that could jeopardize whatever position you're in. Okay?"

She exhaled and nodded.

"What do you want to do the most?" he asked, folding thick arms over a broad chest.

"Check on my mom to make sure she's alright," she said without thinking. Talking to Rowan was easy, a little too easy. She said things that could get her in trouble.

"Where is she?" he continued, unfazed by the new information. There was a casual confidence about Rowan Firebrand that lowered her guard more than it should.

"In a rehab facility, north of Denver," she said, figuring there were plenty of those and she'd be fine as long as she provided vague details of her life. "She was in an accident that left her partially paralyzed. She is starting to make progress, though, and it's way too early to think about moving her." She shrugged. "Plus, I have no idea where I would take her or how to go about setting it up without tipping off..."

She stopped right there.

"Is she being watched?" he asked.

"I'm guessing so," she said. "Although, I can't be certain."

His eyebrow shot up. "And it's dangerous for you to go near her right now?"

"That's right," she confirmed. Again, she figured it couldn't hurt to give up a little information as long as she didn't get too specific.

"What about a phone call to the rehab facility to check on her?" he asked. "Is that something you can do?"

She held her hands out. "I don't have a cell on me."

He reached inside his pocket and produced a cell. "I do."

She shook her head. The Lieutenant would most likely be checking phone records. If the call could be traced back to Rowan, he'd end up in deep trouble. She couldn't allow it. She could have anyone connecting the two of them. "It's not safe."

"Are you saying what I think you are?" he asked. "The person..." He flashed eyes at her. "The *reason* you're out here could be tapping the phones at the rehab place?"

"That's right," she said. "This person has mad computer skills and resources available."

"Okay," he said. "I see."

No, he didn't, and that was the point. She was leading him down the trail of computer hacker instead of law enforcement.

"I'd like to help you, Tara," he said. "But I'm guessing you won't allow me to."

"What can you possibly do?" she asked, sizing him up. The man seemed so down to earth that it would be impossible for him to be a secret billionaire. Though, she did recognize his last name.

"You do this thing when you lie," he started, catching her gaze and holding onto it.

She stopped and stared at him, trying to figure out how he'd nailed her.

"You bring your hand up to touch the dimple on your chin subconsciously," he continued.

"What makes you so certain?" she asked. *Busted.*

"When you grow up with a whole mess of siblings, you get real good at figuring out whose lying," he explained. "Especially when questions come up like whose handprint is on the wall? Or who took a bite out of the freshly baked pie our mother bought at the store. With all those kids around, there was more trouble than common sense."

"Sounds kind of nice actually," she admitted. "To have so many people who, I'm certain, would have your back if you needed it. I used to watch siblings at the playground. They could pick on each other, but let an outsider try…"

"We built our alliances within the family," he said. "We had to in order to survive or be thrown to the wolves. It could be like living in an episode of survivor."

She laughed despite herself. Or maybe because it was needed to break up some of the tension that had her muscles pulled so taut she thought they might snap.

"Since you're lying about who this person's identity is,

it'll be more difficult for me to help you," he said. "No one knows me or that I'm helping you as far as we know. I can put on a decent disguise so cameras won't be able to get a good look at my face. There's no reason to work alone on this, Tara. If hiding here is any indication, you can't afford to be seen. But I can as long as no one knows me. Let's go see your mom."

Was this man too good to be true?

6

Rowan had no plans to wait for a response, so he started packing up his supplies.

"Why do I suspect you're not going to take no for an answer?" Tara asked, a hint of amusement in her voice.

"Because you need the help and, frankly, it'll be boring as hell out here once you leave," he said, trying to infuse some humor into the situation. It worked. She cracked a smile even though she probably wished she could remain stoic.

"You must be one of those adrenaline junkies," she quipped, shaking her head.

"Maybe," he said. "But you could use a friend right now."

"What about the reason you came up here in the first place?" she asked. "Remember that? Because you have stuff to figure out that has nothing to do with the mess my life has become."

"It can wait," he countered. "Besides, being alone with my thoughts doesn't sound as appealing as it did when I took off from the ranch. Now, I think that overly focusing on a problem never did solve it."

"I can't argue that I come up with some of my best solutions when I shift my attention away from a problem," she said before issuing a sigh. "Since you're determined to put yourself in harm's way for me, what can I do to help?"

"Think about what you're hungry for when we stop for lunch," he said. "Denver is a ways away from here."

"Can we do a drive-through somewhere? Anywhere?" she asked. The panic in her voice sounded very real.

"We can do whatever makes you feel safer," he reassured. "To be transparent, I have no intention of letting anything happen to you while you're with me."

She shot him a look. "You don't know what you're getting yourself into."

"Enlighten me," he said as he gathered up supplies and tore down the tent. The great part about the equipment he'd brought was that it was lightweight and could be setup or broken down in a matter of minutes.

"That was fast," Tara marveled, sitting back on her heels as she stayed close to what used to be the fire. He could admit to puffing his chest out a little at the compliment.

"Ready to head down the mountain where my vehicle is parked?" he asked with a smile.

"As much as I'll ever be," she said, wringing her hands together. "It might be best for all of us to get out of the forest anyway. What can I carry?"

"Everything fits inside the rucksack," he said, hoisting the bag on his back before shrugging into the straps. "It's as simple as this."

"I've never been much of a camper," she admitted. "Always wondered why anyone would do this rather than pay for a hotel room down the mountain."

"Now?"

"After last night, I can see where this might be nice under the right circumstances," she said. "The food has been amazing and waking up far away from everyday noises is peaceful." She skipped over the part where she'd been scared to death most of the evening, but he understood what she was saying in the general sense. "It was nice to be far away from everything. No TVs. No cell phones. No contact with anyone else."

"Being alone out here with the stars can be an incredible experience," he said. "I've gotten soft, though. I used to spend more nights outdoors. Now, I'm used to a real bed and a proper kitchen." He laughed. It was contagious. The sound of hers was better than a spring breeze on a hot day.

"I've lived in Colorado my entire life and never once went camping," she said, bemused.

"With all this beauty around you?"

"I've heard of people who live by the beach but they get so used to it they never go there anymore," she said. "I always thought that was strange until I really thought about this being no different. I've done day hikes with my mom but that's the extent of it."

"Don't tell me that you live in ski paradise and don't do that either," he said, incredulous.

"You wouldn't either, if you heard all the news about folks flying off the mountain, falling hundreds of feet to their death on a regular basis," she informed him.

"I doubt I'd watch the news at all," he said. "Folks make their own destiny. Do foolish things, and there are more ways to accidentally kill yourself than stars on a clear night."

"People can be reckless," she said.

"I'm sure you hear of car crashes too, but that doesn't stop you from driving," he continued, feeling on a roll.

"That is true," she said, tensing up. He'd struck a nerve unintentionally. It dawned on him why. Her mom's car wreck. "I have more practice behind the wheel though, so I feel safer. Plus, there's a whole lot of safety features just in case. On a mountain, you're on your own."

"Fair point," he conceded. "Skiing is no different. The more you practice, the more comfortable you feel. Problems happen when folks bite off more than they can chew. They take on a black diamond when they should stick to greens."

"People can accidentally end up on a black diamond," she defended. "Take a wrong turn and then not be able to stop through no fault of their own."

Rowan had a feeling they'd stopped talking about skiing a few minutes ago. This felt more like life. Or more specifically, her life. But he could also relate considering his present circumstances.

How messed up was it that he didn't know if he was going to be a father? Worse yet, his reaction to the pregnancy news had sent Alicia running. She had to resurface at some point, right?

The fact he was here instead of tracking her down told him that he wasn't quite ready for the paternity answer. Because if there was even the slightest chance the kid was his, he had to know how he felt about fatherhood first.

"Tell me what you're thinking," Tara said, cutting into his thoughts.

"My brain is circling back to our earlier conversation," he said. "Wondering whether or not I'm going to be a father."

"The odds are in your favor," she pointed out. "Didn't you say there was less than one percent chance or something like that?"

"Why is it so hard to focus on the ninety-nine percent chance that I'm not?"

"Because you're an honorable person," she said. "You take your responsibilities seriously and would never turn your back on your own flesh and blood. You would also make an amazing father, by the way."

"How could you possibly know that?" he asked. She'd known him for less than twenty-four hours.

"It's easy to see," she said. "You're kind to a fault." She motioned toward his rucksack. "Case in point, you're willing to turn your plans upside down to help a complete stranger who showed up in the worst shape last night unexpectedly."

"I already told you that was a selfish move on my part," he insisted.

"Right," she said. "And I have a bridge for sale."

"Okay," he said. "Maybe I'm inconveniencing myself a little bit by changing my plans. So what? They weren't exactly solid plans anyway. Plus, between having all males on both sides of the family, the ranch is in good hands until I get back."

"You care about hurting other people's feelings," she continued.

"Now, I know you're dreaming."

"It's true," she defended. "You wouldn't be here if that wasn't the case. You're conflicted about your family situation, a family you care very much about."

"Now you're a mind reader?"

"Tell me you don't care about your siblings or cousins," she demanded, her lips in a pout that made him want to haul her against a tree and claim them as his own. Since he wasn't a caveman and consent was king, he wouldn't, but that didn't stop the desire from building. If she knew those feelings, she wouldn't be talking up what a good human he was right now.

"Of course, I care," he said. "Like I told you. We've had to stick together to stand up to our parents."

"Face it, you love your family," she said. "Plus, you're conflicted about having a child with someone you don't love."

"Damn," he said. "That part is true enough."

"It's written all over your face," she said.

"Guess I shouldn't play you in poker," he quipped.

"Probably not a good idea for either of us," she said. "I've gotten so good at hiding my feelings, no one ever calls me out anymore. Except you today. You saw right through me."

"Maybe you finally let your guard down," he said. "Let me in." He paused for a beat. "I have a feeling no one gets past your walls unless you let them."

His words were meant to reassure her, but they seemed to have the opposite effect. She drew back like someone had thrown a punch.

"I didn't mean—"

"No," she cut him off. "Don't do that. It's fine."

Those last two words were always a bad sign. He had no idea what he'd just done wrong or why it gutted him.

∾

Tara was too lax. Rowan was right about one thing. No one got past her walls that she didn't invite inside. She'd gotten so good at keeping everyone away too.

The thought of seeing her mom again, knowing she was okay had made her soft. Her problems were serious. Her life was on the line. Who would take care of her mom if something happened to Tara?

The Lieutenant would hold her accountable for his cousin's death. Did hold her accountable, she corrected.

Rowan was being kind, and it was throwing her off her game. The best way to keep everyone out of harm's way was to maintain her façade, not let anyone get too close, and never discuss what had happened or bring anyone else into the picture.

Last night was the first good night of sleep she'd had since being on the run. She would see her mom, make certain everything was fine and still on track with her healing, and then find a better hiding spot. She could wait this out, right?

All she needed was to buy some time while her mom healed. She would heal. There was no other option.

A tear escaped, sliding down her cheek. It was warm against her cold skin. The droplet fell onto the warm flannel shirt she used as a jacket. It belonged to Rowan and had his male, spicy scent all over it. A scent that was now all over her.

She shoved the thought to the back burner where it simmered.

Her mom was still young. The tragedy that nearly took her life had robbed her ability to walk and speak clearly, for the time being at least. A head injury was a strange thing, the doctor had said. Healing could be slow. Doctor Lewis had said there was no timetable but that she would do everything possible to get Tara's mom walking and speaking again.

The woman who'd been an independent force could no longer speak up for herself, which broke Tara's heart. If the accident had happened a couple of weeks ago instead of last month, Tara would believe the Lieutenant had ordered it to punish her. The timing didn't match up. Her mom's car had been T-boned at an intersection on her way home from the grocery store. According to witnesses, the light was still green when her mom's car was hit. An SUV against a subcompact was no match. Her mom's car had been on the losing side of the equation.

Life could be cruel. Tara had learned the lesson early on after being taken away from an abusive mother, or so her file had said. The woman who was supposed to love and protect her had ignored and punished her instead. Kneeling on rice, with her hands in prayer position, had been one of her birth mother's crueler punishments. Then there was being locked in a closet for an entire weekend with only cups of applesauce being tossed in every once in a while.

Someone, a caring neighbor or teacher—Tara was never told who—had taken pity and called Child Protective Services. Now that was a laughable name for the organization that had ripped her from everything she'd known and handed her over to awful family after awful family. Tara had been thrown to the wolves. As it turned out, becoming a foster meant a monthly check to some folks and not much else. In some cases, she was neglected. In others, she didn't want to think about the abuse she'd endured. She was sure that there were better families out there, but she'd not seen them. That is, until Grace Goodman and her husband. Mr. Goodman died within a year of Tara coming to live with the couple. Their only attempt at biological parenting had ended with a tubal pregnancy that almost took Grace's life. Her husband Rudy said that was all it took for him to know he didn't need children if it meant risking his wife's life.

Tara had never known that kind of unconditional love before. The night she heard that story, she cried herself to sleep. Rudy had been a good person. One she wished she'd had more time to get to know.

Grace had been just as devoted to him. After his death, she never dated or remarried. Said she'd already had the best. Said no one would ever be able to match the kind of love they'd shared and had no plans to settle for less.

Xander would have slipped past Grace's radar too. At least, until it was too late. But then, he'd been the perfect date in the early weeks of their relationship. He'd been charming and attentive. Grace had given a thumbs up after being introduced but Tara wasn't certain her mom understood what was happening.

"Do you need a break?" Rowan asked, cutting into her heavy thoughts. If she lived a hundred years, she would never understand why she'd fallen for a man so willing to throw her under the bus to save his own skin.

"I'm okay," she reassured. "Unless you need to stop." He was the one carrying all the gear.

"Nope," he said. "You've been quiet."

"Thinking," she admitted.

"Anything you want to talk about?" he asked.

Should she trust him? Could she?

It occurred to Tara that she was about to take him to the rehab facility that housed her mother. She was giving him a view into her life. At this point, holding out all the way seemed more than a little silly.

"I'd just turned fifteen years old when my parents took me in," she began. "And was a complete mess after being bounced around in the system."

"How did you end up in foster care to begin with?" he asked. "If you don't mind discussing it."

"That's a long story," she said. "The short version is that I had a deadbeat dad who I don't know and a mom who thought kneeling on rice for hours and being locked in the closet for an entire weekend was appropriate punishment for a five-year-old."

"Damn," he said. "I can't imagine what that must have been like for you."

"It wasn't great," she offered. "The best part about it was that I survived."

"But you went into the system," he said.

"Spent the next ten years being bounced around," she explained. "Let's just say the interesting houses used an electrical cord against the backs of my thighs for punishment."

"Those folks should be strung up and shown what it feels like," he said through clenched teeth.

"In ten years, I was bounced six times," she said. "I'd developed an attitude that didn't help matters, if I'm being totally honest. My grades were just good enough to keep me from getting kicked out of school without exerting any real energy studying."

"School wasn't exactly my favorite place," Rowan said.

"Mine either, except that it was better than most of the places I lived," she admitted. "I turned fifteen and my social worker was getting pretty worn out by me. Looking back, she was one of my biggest champions, even if I couldn't see it back then."

"I have yet to meet a teenager in the right state of mind," he said.

"All those hormones, right?" she asked, but it was more statement than question.

"Exactly," he agreed. "The only good thing about those few years of pimples and insecurities is that they don't last long."

"I have a hard time believing you were anything but

perfect as a teenager," she quipped. "Football quarterback who dated the cheerleading captain in the glory of Friday night lights and all that."

He just laughed and shook his head. "Not exactly but go on."

"Anger would be a good word to describe my state of mind at that point," she said. "I'd been in and out of juvie for doing things I had no business doing. Like setting a neighbor's garbage can on fire and stealing candy bars and makeup from stores. Nothing big, just always in trouble."

"Sounds like you were just looking for attention any way you could get it," he surmised.

"The funny thing is that I didn't see it that way," she said. "When I didn't get caught, I believed I was getting back at the 'system' that was hurting me, tossing me around to different people not caring what they sent me into." She paused. "Now, I know that I was only hurting myself but, hey, that took years to figure out."

"Did you meet your mother at fifteen?" he asked.

"Grace Goodman is my foster, but she's my mother for all intents and purposes," she said. "She's the only person I would ever call mom. The person who gave birth to me doesn't deserve the title. And I know people disagree with that sentiment. I've heard friends talking to each other, giving each other advice, which is always telling them to call the person who gave birth to them. Why? Relationships are a two-way street. I have no interest in chasing someone or giving them props for the simple fact they have a uterus. Being a mom is so much more than birthing someone. Does that make sense?"

Rowan grunted. He, of all people, would understand where she was coming from. "It resonates more than you know."

"Grace is special to me," she said, hearing the reverence in her own voice. "If not for her and Rudy, I'd probably be in prison right now."

Those words got a reaction out of Rowan. Had she shared too much?

7

Tara was finally opening up to Rowan. Could he get her to trust him?

"What do you do for a living?" he asked as they neared the bottom of the mountain, trudging through the fresh snow. Talking on the way down made the time zip by as he watched for other footprints.

"I own a small dog grooming business," she said, with more than a hint of pride in her voice. "I have a storefront in a popular strip mall and eight part-time employees." She hesitated. "Ever notice how much easier it is to be around animals than people sometimes?"

"Yes," he said with a chuckle. "Sounds like you turned your life around after getting an unfair shake early on."

"My criminal record was sealed after I turned eighteen," she said. "It's the only reason I got a second chance in life, which I wouldn't have had without Grace and Rudy."

"You made a success out of yourself," he pointed out. "Most people don't change even when given a new lease on life."

"Sometimes your background catches up to you," she

said on a sharp sigh. He quickly realized there was more to the story.

"I'm parked over here," he said as they crossed the lot at the base of the mountain. There were a couple of vehicles parked in the lot this morning. Had folks decided to go up after the storm had passed? He surveyed them to make certain no one was inside or paying close attention to the two of them.

They were on the road not ten minutes later after plugging the address into GPS, warming up with the heater, and peeling off their outer layers. Tara rubbed her hands together in front of the vent to warm them faster.

"Tell me more about this background and what kind of threat you're up against," he said.

She started to protest but then clamped her mouth closed.

"All I'm trying to do is assess the damage here," he explained. "See what kinds of resources we might need to help you out of this."

"I can't leave Grace," she said. "I'm all she has now."

"Which is why it's even more important for you to talk to me," he said. "I want to help."

Several quiet moments ticked by. At this point, he would lose if he spoke first. She needed time. He would give it to her. Rather than push, he tapped his thumb on the steering wheel and headed toward the highway.

"She's all I have too," Tara finally said.

"You have me now," he said. "At least temporarily, until you and Grace are reunited and safe."

"This is all my fault," she said. "I had no idea the guy I was in a relationship with was related to someone involved in a crime ring."

"Why not?" he asked, curious as to how that could be

hidden if two people were in love. Then again, Alicia had tried to deceive him about something as important as fatherhood.

"For starters, he was a cop," she said, twisting her fingers together.

"Was?"

"He came at me, desperate," she said. "Things between us had been falling apart for a while. His cousin asked a favor."

"Your boyfriend couldn't refuse?" Rowan asked, not liking using the word 'boyfriend' when it came to her.

"This guy who goes by the name Lieutenant, did a little digging into my personal life it seems," she said. "He told Xander using my shop to launder money wasn't a request and that someone with my background shouldn't have a problem with bending the law. Said I wouldn't be involved and that all I had to do was look the other way."

"I can probably guess how that went over with you," he said, thinking not too well.

"Obviously, I wouldn't do it," she continued, folding her arms across her chest. "Sometimes I think it would be a whole lot easier if I'd gone along with the whole situation. Maybe it would have been less messy and I wouldn't be in the position of not being able to see my mom. She must think something awful happened to me since I abruptly stopped coming."

"What stopped you from turning a blind eye?" he asked. "Other than the fact it was illegal and you could risk being busted, losing your shop, and possibly going to jail."

"Believe me, I thought about every one of those things," she said. "But my first thought was Rudy." She turned to look out the passenger side window and sniffed. "I made a promise to him on his deathbed that I would only do things that would make him and Grace proud of me. I said I would take care of Grace and then I told him that he could go. Grace would always be safe with me. How could I go back on that?"

"You couldn't," he agreed. He respected her even more now that he knew the reason she couldn't compromise. A person was only as good as their word. Her past didn't have to dictate her future, but he understood how other people would view the situation. See her as guilty because of her past despite how much she'd turned her life around. She was right. Once people got an idea stuck in their head, it was next to impossible to change their minds. He'd lived that his entire life being a Firebrand from the 'wrong' side of the family.

"You said going to law enforcement isn't an option," he said. "Why not?"

"Because I don't know who the Lieutenant is and he would take it out on Grace," she immediately responded. "He told me as much when he called me, which was the reason I disappeared. I panicked, wanted more time. I've given this a lot of thought and still can't seem to come up with a good answer."

"Was that the reason you ditched your phone?" he asked.

"They can't find me if it's not with me," she said. "He told me point blank not to go to the law or Grace would pay the price."

The saying *caught between a rock and a hard place* applied here.

"Plus, I just killed someone and that will be made to look like my fault. They'll ruin me and my reputation," she added.

Did Rowan hear correctly? He shook his head to clear

the cobwebs. He must have heard wrong. "Hold on there a minute. Did you say that you just killed someone?" Flashbacks to his mother's arrest and guilty plea slammed into him.

"In self-defense," Tara said. "Yes, I did." She sniffed a few more times, keeping her face turned toward the side where he couldn't get a good look.

"How?" he asked, remembering how quick she'd been with his knife along with the blood on her arms. "You need to explain the situation to me or I don't know how I'll be able to help you." The term *accomplice* came to mind. He was a lone camper who'd decided to stick it out during a storm that had caused most to scatter down the mountain. And then he just happened to be in the right place to help her last night. There wasn't a jury in the state who would believe him. Plenty of hikers saw him going up the mountain when everyone else was coming down.

Tara was right about one thing, this situation had *trouble* written all over it.

She reached into her back pocket and produced a rock with a jagged edge. "I slammed this into his temple."

The murder weapon was on her person? There would be trace amounts of blood on it. This would be a slam dunk case for any prosecutor worth his salt.

"I've been hiding in an abandoned cabin near the forest," she said, holding out her left arm. She rolled up the sleeve, revealing a bruise the size of a grapefruit. "He found me but I got away."

"The next time we stop, I'd like to take pictures of your bruise," he said through clenched teeth. Rowan realized he was white-knuckling the steering wheel, so he forced his fingers to relax. "We need to gather all the proof we can to substantiate your story."

"Okay," she said after a thoughtful pause.

"Sounds like you could go into witness protection," he pointed out. "Would that be so terrible?"

"What about Grace?" she asked.

"I would think she could go too, but I'll admit that I have no idea how it works," he said. "It seems like the two of you could start over together somewhere."

Tara tapped her fingers on the armrest. "How difficult would it be to find her now that she's been in the accident?"

He couldn't help but ask the next question. "Was it, though? Or was it some kind of twisted warning?"

"The other person in the wreck sadly didn't make it," she said. "My heart goes out to the family for their loss. But it's not like we can ask the driver."

"We could go to the family," he said. "Someone might know something or be willing to talk. They might want the bastards who put their loved one up to ramming their vehicle into someone else to pay."

"I guess enough time has passed," she reasoned. "I'm sure they're still in mourning but they might want to unburden themselves of information like this. But we could be barking up the wrong tree and cause more pain to a family that doesn't deserve it."

"As much as I hate the thought, we are short on options," he said. "I wouldn't suggest it if there were other trails to follow."

"Okay," she said on a sharp sigh. "Let's think about it. I have their names somewhere at home if we decide to go down that route." She gasped. "It can't be safe for us to go there. If any place is being watched, it'll be my apartment."

"The blood on your arms," he said, circling back because he needed to understand what happened last night. "Who does it belong to?"

"Xander," she said low and under her breath. "I killed a cop, Rowan. No one will believe I acted in self-defense." She brought her hand up to bite on her thumbnail.

"I believe you," he said, reaching over to squeeze her hand in reassurance. She was right, though, this situation had gone from bad to worse in a tail's shake.

"The irony is that I got away with so much when I was young. Not everything, of course, But most of it. And now, I'll go to prison for the rest of my life for something I didn't do. At least not on purpose." She worked the thumb, so he reached over and gently removed her hand from the vicinity of her teeth before she brought blood. "The reason I didn't want you anywhere near me is because I'm going to be labeled a cop killer and you're going to go down as my accomplice."

"I won't," he reassured despite considering the possibility already. There was another irony here in the fact he'd bolted out of Texas to avoid thinking about a murder case only to find himself knee-deep in one in Colorado. "At best, I'll be seen as a good Samaritan who helped someone after a bad storm in the mountains. Folks come here to escape a whole lot of situations. And, sometimes like in my case, to clear their heads. It's as simple as that."

"That would explain last night and helping me down the mountain today," she said. "It doesn't cover checking on my mom or driving me around today."

"Why not?" he asked. "You got separated from your ride on the mountain in a storm. It happens."

"Okay," she agreed. "I'll give you that. Except you know the truth about me and I would never expect you to lie."

"Believe me when I say that I can afford an attorney," he said, realizing he might need one if this thing went south.

She shot him a look that he could have felt a mile away.

"You can't possibly be rich. Right? You said you were a cattle rancher. I've vaguely heard of your last name. But I won't have you spending your hard-earned money on a lawyer, just because you decided to help me."

Rowan laughed. He couldn't help himself.

"What part of that is funny?" she asked, defensively.

She had no idea how much money his family could throw at a lawyer and not miss for a second. Should he tell her? Would she look at him the same?

8

"You'd probably have to know my family to truly understand why I would laugh, but I couldn't stop myself. I promise my intention wasn't to offend you."

Rowan's explanation caused more questions to surface. Tara appreciated his kindness up to this point. The man was in over his head. She needed him to understand how hopeless it was to continue to help her. And yet, she couldn't do any of this without him. She had no cell phone, no vehicle, and her home most certainly was being watched. Show her face there, and she'd be dead in a heartbeat. If the Lieutenant's people didn't kill her, the cops might.

There was no way she was going to spend the rest of her life in jail. She wouldn't be able to help her mom if Tara was locked behind bars.

It would be so easy if she could bring in the cops, like Rowan had suggested. Except that she'd killed one of their own, self-defense or not, and wouldn't be safe anywhere. She could leave the state and not outrun the title of cop killer. A manhunt would be underway the minute Xander's body is found. She'd been talked out of filing domestic abuse charges after he landed a flat-palmed smack on her left cheek. He hit her so hard it almost felt like her eyeball would pop out. It took a few minutes to shake off the shock and feel the pain. Officer Jenn McNeely had explained how the brotherhood among officers still worked. The female officer disliked the term 'brotherhood' but said law enforcement in Denver was slow to change.

"I didn't earn the bulk of my wealth independently," Rowan finally said, interrupting her heavy thoughts. "It has all been handed to me as a birthright. Which means, I didn't deserve it. So, I only spend what I need, which isn't much. The rest is sitting in a bank account waiting for a good reason to spend it."

"Oh." It wasn't the fanciest reaction, but Tara honestly didn't know what else to say. She felt her jaw fall slack, so she forced her mouth to clamp shut. "I'm sorry. You're down to earth, not exactly the type of person I would expect to have buckets of money hiding in the barn."

He laughed, which broke some of the tension. "I guess not."

"It's just that I noticed how rough your hands are," she pointed out. "You work for a living. Plus, ranching work has got to be one of the most difficult jobs. You look strong and fit." Now, she felt a red blush crawl up her neck. "What I mean to say is that you don't look soft, like I'd expect a rich person to look." Wasn't she putting her foot in her mouth. *Nice job.*

Thankfully, Rowan kept laughing.

"I'm sorry," she said. "I'm not saying any of this the right way."

"You're doing a great job in my book," Rowan said. There was a teasing quality to his voice that made her smile.

"I'm butchering it," she countered. It was good to laugh again. She couldn't remember the last time she could let her guard down even a little bit with someone. Living with Xander over the past six months had caused her to walk on eggshells. She didn't realize until now just how much she'd been watching every word these last few weeks. He'd pressured her more and more as the days passed, saying if she didn't agree that the Lieutenant would come down on him. He'd been told to 'get his woman under control' according to Xander. She'd believed him too.

Xander had put on quite a show. It wasn't until their blowout fight that she'd realized he was going to get a cut. Greed was the real reason he'd been pressuring her. He'd wanted to go into business with the Lieutenant, stating that cops didn't make a fraction of the money common criminals made. There was no sick child or exorbitant medical bills building up in the background that would push Xander to be on the take. He believed the extra money was owed to him since he put his life on the line every day to keep the streets safe. People had turned on cops, or so he'd said, so he felt no need to stay above board with his activities. It had become a dog-eat-dog world where only the strongest survived. That was trash, and he knew it, and she couldn't and wouldn't excuse his behavior.

"I'm flattered," Rowan said, pulling her out of her deep thoughts. "Believe me, there's nothing worse than someone who doesn't know how to roll their sleeves up and get a job done."

"Is your whole family that way?" she asked, nudging the conversation in a new direction.

"I guess you could say the one positive trait we all got was our work ethic," he admitted. "No one is all that enamored with money either. Unless you count my mother."

"I'm truly sorry for that. But try living without it as a kid with no ability to change your circumstances," she noted.

"Damn. You're right," he said. "That made me sound like the biggest jerk."

"No," she said. "It didn't. I admire the fact that you don't run around parading your family money. I wouldn't respect you if you did."

"I'll take that as a compliment," he said with a smile. "I do realize how important it is to have enough money to keep food on the table and a decent roof over a family's head. I didn't mean to come off like I don't appreciate the position I'm in financially."

"It's okay," she reassured. Another thought occurred to her that Alicia might have been after some of that family money with the pregnancy. Tara tabled the idea for the time being but planned to bring it up again when the time was right.

"It's tricky when you didn't earn the money on your own terms," he continued. She could imagine that to be true. He was the kind of person who would want to make his own mark on the world. Was it part of the reason he was considering leaving the ranch he obviously loved to start a business with his friend? She banked that question, too. For now.

"I have to say there hasn't been a day that goes by that I don't wish a million dollars dropped in my lap," she admitted. "Legally, of course."

He didn't respond.

"Money can solve a lot of problems," she said.

"It doesn't fix everything," he pointed out. "It doesn't make your parents get along or your grandfather a nice man. In fact, the opposite can be true. Folks can show their true colors when their bank account is full. And in my mother's case, it's never enough. You'd be surprised at the lengths folks will go to in order to get money." He tapped the steering wheel with the palm of his hand. "Strike that last comment. You of all people do know, considering all that you've been and still are going through."

She couldn't agree more. "It can bring out the worst in people."

"My theory is that money isn't bad," he reasoned. "It's not really more than numbers in a bank account, right?"

"True," she said tentatively.

"My belief is that people act their true self when they have money and don't need anything from anyone else," he stated. "I guess I always knew who I wanted to be. I'm a rancher through and through. I like the outdoors. There's nothing better than a sky full of stars on a clear night. Money can't buy those things."

"That is true," she agreed, thinking he'd just answered his question about going into business with his buddy. "I guess I've never had enough to worry about how it might change me." She was being honest. "My shop does well, which means we make payroll, can pay rent, and I'm able to save up enough to buy a small house. My car is almost paid off, so I'd planned to keep driving it a few more years. It still has miles left on it. And I wanted to bring Grace home to live in my guestroom once I closed on the house. Xander promised to give me a cut of the money, like I needed a shortcut or would jeopardize my livelihood to make a quick buck. He said he could skim some off the top and no one would know." She shook her head. "When I refused, he said I was putting his life on the line and that he'd made promises."

"You were in a difficult spot," he said. "I admire you for

not caving when most would roll over with demands like that."

"I have blood on my hands, Rowan."

She meant that statement literally and figuratively.

"No, you don't," he said. "You mentioned self-defense. I know you don't think anyone would believe you—"

"They won't need to," she cut him off. "I'll be dead before the law can protect me to shut me up. The Lieutenant won't be thrilled with me, knowing I could turn state's witness to save my own hide, now that I'll be billed as a cop killer." This was one in a long list of dangers. "And what if they look into Xander's personal life? They'll probably discover his relationship with the Lieutenant through his brother. Xander was most likely on the take now that I really think about it. This couldn't be the first time he'd ever planned to skim money."

"That will be your defense," Rowan pointed out. "Once the law sees how dirty Xander was, they'll have to believe you."

"Spoken like someone who has always been treated fairly by the judicial system," she said. "I won't be so lucky."

"Because of your background?" he asked.

"That's right," she confirmed. "If people can find anything in your past to dig up and get people to focus on, it's over for your reputation."

"That, I do understand," he said. "It's a shame."

"But it's true," she said. "There's no hope for someone like me once Xander's body is found."

"Are you certain he's dead?"

"There was so much blood," she said. "I checked for a pulse and didn't find one."

Rowan gripped the steering wheel tighter as he turned into the parking lot of the rehab center. "We're here."

9

Rowan wasn't sure what he was thinking by pulling directly into the parking lot of the five-story brick façade rehab center. He circled once and then exited, having lost count of the number of vehicles there. The building was hopping with outpatient activity. The center was larger than he'd assumed it would be. "We should probably come up with a plan before one of us heads inside."

"They'll recognize me inside there," Tara said. "It's not safe for me to go. Will you?"

"I'd be happy to step in," he confirmed. People coming and going might make it easier to slip inside. "Give me the details about logistics of the place. But first, let's take those pictures of your bruises. We need to gather as much evidence as possible to corroborate your story."

He got out his camera, and snapped the pics with clenched teeth. It was hard to look at the evidence of abuse without being able to do a damn thing anything about it. He issued a sharp sigh when they were done. "This never should have happened."

"It's the reason I started taking self-defense," she said.

He nodded. There was a whole lot more he could say but they needed to stay focused. "What am I walking into in there?"

"There's a long counter when you first enter, almost like a nurse's station," she began. "To your right, there will be a set of glass doors that automatically swish open but you'll need to be allowed in. Either the person working the desk can do it or someone can tap their ID badge to get the doors to open. The right side is for inpatient care. The left side has a big lobby but that's for outpatient."

"Do you have access without a badge?" he asked.

She shook her head as he pulled into the grocery store parking lot down the street.

"We'll have to finagle your way past the desk," she said on a shrug. "I'm not exactly sure the best way to get that done."

"I have an idea," he said before exiting the truck. He rounded the front of the vehicle to open Tara's door. She beat him to the punch but didn't exit.

"Okay if I stay here?" she asked. "There's a slim chance someone might recognize me, but it wouldn't be smart to get this far, only to be identified. Plus, we have no idea if I'm wanted by the law at this point."

"Agreed," he said. "I'm not sure what I was thinking. It's best if you stay here and stay low." He tapped the window with his knuckle. "Be careful, okay?"

She sucked in a breath and nodded before closing her door. The snick of a lock came a few seconds later.

Once inside the grocery, Rowan turned to his right where the floral department had a variety of bouquets. He bought a large one, using cash so he couldn't be traced back to this store, in case anyone was watching. He had no idea how far the reach of the criminal involved might be. Tara was right, though. Having her out here running around loose meant someone could testify against them. This increased the likelihood they would have eyes on her mother's rehab facility. If not full-time, then either have someone on the inside report activity or patrol past to keep watch on the place.

He grabbed the flower arrangement and then started toward the truck. As he walked toward the glass double doors, he caught sight of a ballcap. It might be nice to wear since he could keep his head bowed, which would keep his face hidden and out of view from any security cameras at the rehab center. Doubling back to make another purchase would only keep him away from Tara another couple of minutes. He could risk it for the extra protection.

The floral arrangement was large enough to cover his face when he walked up to the counter she'd described, but cameras would most likely be mounted in the corners of the room from the ceiling. If he could sweet talk the front desk into letting him deliver the flowers personally, he would be able to check on Grace Goodman's condition. It occurred to him that Tara might be able to call for an update, since she would be listed as next of kin. But she didn't want to surface yet.

His racing pulse calmed down a couple of notches when he got back to the truck and saw Tara slouched in the passenger seat.

"These lilies are my mom's favorites," Tara said as she took the vase from him and positioned it between her thighs for extra stability. It would hide her face from oncoming traffic, an added benefit since no one should recognize him. The window on the passenger side was the main vulnerability at this point. It was an acceptable risk with the bouquet. She could easily turn her head toward him if needed to shield her profile from folks in vehicles that pulled up alongside them.

Rowan reclaimed the driver's seat and then navigated onto the roadway. He reached over and touched her hand before returning his to the wheel at the stoplight. "Part of me doesn't like you anywhere near the rehab center."

"We can always park across the street," she offered. It was obvious from the sound of her voice that she was on edge. The idea might make his delivery guy persona less believable. But that didn't matter right now. He wanted her as far away from the building as possible.

"You'll stay inside the truck?" he asked.

"Just like at the grocery store," she reassured. "I can get behind the wheel if you like, in case you need a fast pickup."

"That's not a bad idea actually," he said. "I'll leave the key with you, so you can bolt if you need to. If you're in danger, don't worry about me. Just take off. Okay?"

She was fiercely shaking her head no. "I won't do that. I won't leave you."

"I'd be better off if you did," he felt the need to point out. It was partially true. "Promise me that you'll take care of you first. I come second."

"You've been too kind for me to strand you," she said. The soft nature of her voice hit him square in the chest. It was rare she showed her vulnerability. Doing so brought out all his protective instincts. "But you might want to rethink being associated with me. This could be your last chance to distance yourself."

"All I have to say is that someone hopped inside my truck," he continued, needing to convince her. "I'll say you drove off and I have no idea who is behind the wheel."

She was quiet this time, which meant he was starting to get through. He took it as a sign to continue.

"I'll put on an award-winning performance if it makes you feel better," he said. "That way, no one will put together the two of us as being in league. It'll make it easier for me to move around. Although, I'd be watched for a few days so I'd need you to stay away. Think you can do that?"

"Where would I go, Rowan?"

"Anywhere else but here," he said. "Ditch the truck as soon as it's safe and go in the opposite direction anyone would guess." He fished out his cell from the front pocket of his jeans. "Take this." He handed it over, wishing he'd thought to buy a burner phone. There were so many ways in which this could go south. Part of him thought maybe they should retreat and regroup. Think all of this through before making a move. Except that could give this Lieutenant time to swoop in and kidnap her mom. Rowan muttered a curse.

Tara took the offering. Her fingers grazed his palm, sending a jolt of electricity racing up his arm straight to his heart. He'd never experienced anything so powerful from such a simple touch.

The urge to lean into the cabin of the truck, across the seat, and not stop until he'd claim those pink lips of hers was almost overwhelming. He wouldn't do it, of course. Tara needed something that had been in short supply during her life...a friend.

He admired and respected her courage. Even now, when the deck was stacked against them, she kept her chin up. There was a vulnerability in her eyes that made him wish he could take all of this away, give her the life she deserved.

There was a long list of her other positive attributes, which also made him realize she was one of a kind. Not many folks could rise up out of a horrific start in life and do better. His mind snapped to his mother's situation. She'd also been to hell and back when she was young. Seeing the similarities in backgrounds and the differences in how each had dealt with adversity gave him even more respect for Tara. She wasn't the norm. His mother had learned to live with her circumstances, hide from them, but she never seemed to conquer them. Different personalities? Tara and Jackie Firebrand couldn't be more opposite.

It was only recently that he'd learned about his mother's troubled past. As much as he didn't see it as a 'get out of jail free' card, in a manner of speaking, he was also starting to see how it would take an incredibly strong-minded person to be able to overcome an abusive childhood.

"Be careful in there," Tara said before meeting him in the middle and pressing a kiss to his lips. The simple act shouldn't send fire coursing through his veins in the way it did. It shouldn't make him feel like he was suddenly missing out on something important in his life. It shouldn't make him ache in a way he'd never known before.

It did.

Holy hell. He took in a deep breath and caught her gaze. Her eyes glittered with something that looked a lot like need. His body reacted. Every muscle in his body chorded. The coil in his chest tightened. Tara held the key for release.

One small kiss had never threatened to obliterate his resolve in the way this one just did. Part of him wanted to dive in headfirst and see where this could go with Tara. Part of him knew better than to get too involved with someone else facing jailtime, while he had so much drama going on back at home and especially while her future was so uncertain. Part of him wanted to run for the hills because he was already knee-deep in courtrooms and plea deals. Taking a break from Lone Star Pass wasn't exactly moving him away from everything he'd been trying to escape at home.

Maybe that was the point. Maybe he was supposed to stick around and see it through. Maybe he should have turned around and gone back at the halfway point on the drive to Colorado.

Except he couldn't regret his choice to continue on, because it was the reason he was here with Tara right now.

What was he supposed to do with that?

∼

Tara swallowed to ease the sudden dryness in her throat. She hadn't planned on leaning into Rowan and kissing him, but she'd been thinking about doing it all day. If they'd met at another time and another place, he was exactly the kind of person she would like to get to know.

She almost laughed out loud at the thought. There wasn't a world in which the two of them would have met. He was escaping home and she was running from her past and present. The fact their paths had collided at all was the mother of all coincidences.

Not that it mattered now because she needed to get him up to speed on what he was about to walk into.

After a deep breath, she began, "Mom's room is on the second floor. You already know how challenging it'll be to get past the front desk. Once inside, there is a set of stairs next to the elevator. I'd take the stairs if I were you."

He nodded. His face of hard angles and planes was back to being all business. The depths of desire she'd seen in his sea-blue eyes a moment ago nearly robbed her ability to breathe.

"Stairs," he said, "got it."

"Mom's room number is 222," she said, doing her best to shove those other thoughts aside. It was go time. There was no room for error or distraction, no matter how gorgeous Rowan Firebrand might be. His intelligence made him even more handsome, which felt impossible given how beautiful the man was already.

"Easy enough to remember," he reasoned.

"I wish I had a picture of her," she said. "It would make this a whole lot easier if you knew who you were looking for. We don't look alike."

"Give me a rundown on the basics," he said.

"She's in her late sixties," Tara informed. "But she looks more like mid-fifties, I'd say. She's about five feet-five-inches. She used to be a runner a long time ago, until she developed plantar fasciitis. She would be considered slim by most standards. A small to medium shirt size with size five pants."

"Hair color?" he asked, taking all the information in. His gaze unfocused like he was looking inside himself. She realized he was painting a picture in his mind that he would no doubt commit to memory.

"Blonde," she said. "Not platinum but a soft natural blonde with blue eyes. Not like yours, though. Yours are like looking into the sea, whereas hers are more of a cobalt blue." Tara could feel the red blush crawling up her neck at the mention of his eyes.

"Would she be wearing her own clothes or hospital gown?" he asked. It was a fair question because the rehab facility had a hospital feel.

"Her own clothes," she said. "Which would be lounge pants and a t-shirt most likely."

"Will I scare her by walking in her room?"

"It's possible," she said. "I hope not. I haven't been by so all you have to do is say you're a friend of mine. You should be okay."

"So, she remembers people?" he asked.

"Me? Yes."

"Okay, good," he said, taking the bouquet from her. "I wasn't sure about that, since we're dealing with a traumatic brain injury."

The fact he'd used the word 'we' shouldn't send warmth through her body, beginning at the center of her chest and spreading outward from there to the tips of her fingers.

"Her memory is good," she reassured. "Some of her motor function was affected and her speech is coming back. She remembers her life before the accident. The actual event is a blank, but that's to be expected according to the doctors."

Rowan stared at her for a long moment. He opened his mouth to speak before clamping it shut again.

"What?" she asked.

"Nothing," he said before shaking his head. "It's just that you're memorable."

Well, didn't that comment just spread more of that warmth through her. She knew better than to go there with Rowan. His life was in Texas. Hers was falling apart in Colorado. Not to mention the fact she would likely end up in prison for the rest of her life.

Could she grab her mom and run away? Hide? Or was there no distance the Lieutenant wouldn't go to find her?

"What's that look in your eyes?" Rowan asked. When she looked at him again, she saw that he was studying her.

"What look?"

"The wild one just now," he clarified.

"To be honest, I was just contemplating the odds of

success if I grabbed my mom and made a run for the border," she admitted.

"Which one?" he asked. "Border, I mean?"

"Does it matter?" she asked. "Canada. Mexico. Same difference. The point is that I'd be taking her out of this facility, and we'd find our way out of this mess."

"The crime syndicate you mentioned isn't likely to stop searching for you after you disappear," he said. "You know that, right?"

She didn't respond because she didn't want to listen to logic when her emotions were running wild.

"Not to mention the fact all your problems would just compound the longer you were away," he continued.

Again, she didn't care for reason at this point. She was desperate.

"The Lieutenant will have long arms," he said. "The law will believe you're a cop killer. There'll be no end to your running and you wouldn't be here to defend yourself. Plus you'd be dragging your mom with you. Is that what you want?"

"Well, no," she said. "Of course not. But what else can I do? To your point, the Lieutenant isn't going to leave me alone. And the law will always be after me if I don't end up locked up already." She blew out a frustrated breath. "Xander might have already been found, and it isn't going to look good for me. I'm going to end up serving time for the rest of my life and missing out on time with Mom. Why wouldn't I take off, get new identities for us both, and stay away?"

"Because it's not that simple," he said, his voice calm and reassuring.

"Why not?" she asked, realizing her emotions had taken the wheel a long time ago.

"Like I said, you'll always be running," he pointed out. "Your mom still needs rehab so that limits your possibilities right there plus makes it easier to find you. Is that what you want? To never have a home? To move from town to town under an assumed name?"

"No," she said with a whole lot of anger. "Who would want that? But, maybe that's the best I can do. Maybe that's where life is taking me and I should stop fighting against it and just go with the tide."

"You're a good person, Tara." His voice soothed parts of her that had long since been broken. "You wouldn't like being on the run. Never settling in one spot for long. Even with your mom with you, you'll have to be alone and live a half-life. You deserve so much more than that."

Did she? Because right now she didn't think so even though she might wish for more. He made her wish for more. But there was nothing she could do about it.

10

Rowan stood there at the truck. He would stand there for as long as it took to make Tara see the light. No one deserved the world as much as Tara. The fact she was this devoted to her mom, despite the personal risk, said everything he needed to know about her character.

Tara couldn't get a break. Life hit some people harder than others. He was beginning to see and understand that now.

Same with his mother?

Jackie had certainly gotten the short end of the stick when it came to her parents. The very people who should have loved and protected her were the ones who let an uncle take advantage of her. Granted, they didn't know it was happening. In fact, according to what he'd been told, they couldn't believe it was true. But nothing good had ever come from sticking someone's face in the sand instead of dealing with an issue straight on once they were told. Would his mother have turned out differently if she'd faced her demons rather than allowed them to take the wheel?

Was he being too hard on her?

Life dealt a bad hand to some people. It broke some people. Tara should be broken. And yet, here she was still fighting.

"Do I, Rowan?" Tara asked, breaking through his heavy thoughts. "Does anyone *deserve* anything in this life? Maybe none of us are entitled to a thing. Maybe life wasn't meant to bend to our will. Maybe, it's up to us to learn and grow from every experience."

Those words resonated. They made a whole lot of sense. And he was beginning to think he was the jerk when it came to his mother. Maybe it was his job to at least try to understand what she'd been through and why she'd turned out the way she was. Her life had been hell on wheels. He could only imagine the abuse she'd suffered. He'd experienced something different, neglect. On balance, it was a whole lot better than what his mother had endured. If he and his brothers had been informed about their mother's background, everyone could have been a lot more understanding and forgiving. Their relationships would be different, better. At the very least, they would have been able to offer more compassion when it came to her quirks and the way she dealt with the world.

But then, that would mean handling affairs in a mature, adult manner, which was something his father had never been taught to do. Did the environment in which a person was raised determine how they would deal with life in the future? Did it determine their personality? Or the way they would look at life? Treat others?

Coming from a family of nine boys with a variety of personality types, Rowan didn't buy into someone being pigeonholed from birth based on how they were treated. He could, however, admit their childhood left them all with trust issues. Some to a bigger degree than others. Their upbringing taught them not to believe in others but to rely on themselves. The relationship between their parents definitely made Rowan and his brothers leery of doing long-term with anyone.

"Settling down in one place has never appealed to me," Tara said, breaking through his heavy thoughts.

He was the epitome of being settled. Firebrand Ranch was his home and where he intended to stay once he got his head on straight again. It wasn't for everyone. He needed to reach out to Benny, so he could let his friend know opening a business in Fort Worth wasn't in the cards for Rowan if it meant leaving Lone Star Pass. He would, however, offer to be a silent partner. Funding the operation was good enough for him. It would help Benny get his feed store off the ground, which seemed like a good investment.

"I appreciate what you're saying, though," she continued when he didn't respond. What could he say?

"It's true," he admitted. "You deserve the world."

His comment caused her to blush.

"That, I'm not so sure about," she said. "But I would like to have a stable home for my mom when she's released. I have no idea how long it'll take for her to fully heal or if she'll gain all her mobility back."

He noticed that she steered the conversation toward her mom and away from herself. He went with it. "I could make some calls once it's safe to have her looked at by the best in the field."

"You would do that?" Tara asked, blinking in disbelief.

"It's what ranchers do," he said. "We help each other out."

"I have nothing to offer in return," she said.

"It doesn't work that way," he pointed out. "Think of it like a 'pay it forward' type of thing. When you're in a position to help someone else, move the kindness to them. You don't have to reach back to me. Okay?"

"Got it," she said reluctantly. "And thank you."

"You're welcome," he said before placing the ballcap on his head and then taking the vase. "Let's hope I get past the front desk."

"Fingers crossed," she said. "I'll have your phone, so you won't be able to call out for help. Do you think it's such a good idea to leave it with me? I'll have the truck."

"On second thought," he shifted the heavy vase to the crook of his left arm and then took the cell back. He shoved it inside his pocket. "I might be able to use it as a prop if I get any flack."

"Good luck," she said as she shifted over to the driver's seat.

"Let's hope I won't need it," he said. Luck had never been on his side. It was the reason he'd learned to work hard and leave nothing to chance. Lady Luck was too fickle.

Rowan crossed the street into the back of a fairly busy parking lot. The rehab facility seemed to have a decent amount of both types of patients. There was a handful of folks heading in and out of the front door on crutches or in wheelchairs.

He inconspicuously watched the pattern as he made his way across the lot. Was there a way to schmooze his way past the person behind the counter? The facility used the same lobby for both inpatient and outpatient. Would that help?

An idea struck as a supply van passed between him and the building. The van turned left, heading toward the back.

Was there a backdoor? A dock? There had to be. Building management had to move supplies in some way. They wouldn't want to use the front door with the traffic there. It would be a logistical nightmare.

He picked up the pace to a slight jog, following the van, stopping at the corner of the building. The van had already swiveled around by the time he got there, and was backing up toward a regular metal door.

Could he slip past?

Rowan gaited toward the vehicle, pressing his back against the side of the van when it came to a stop. There was a buzzer by the metal door. The driver stepped out, leaving the van's engine running. He pressed the buzzer and held it to the point of annoying the person on the other side. The door came swinging open and an angry orderly stood there, arms folded across his chest.

The driver mumbled something that sounded like an apology. It appeased the orderly, who took up almost the entire doorframe. He was bald and had a Mr. Clean look to him.

Mr. Clean swatted at empty air before turning his back toward the van and stepping inside. The door, however, was fixed to stay open. Rowan figured this was his best opportunity to make a move. It was now or never.

Before he could talk himself out of the move, he tucked his chin to his chest and headed inside. The best way to succeed was to make it look like he knew what he was doing and where he was going.

He hoped there wouldn't be a point in which he needed an ID badge to access a hallway but he'd cross that bridge when it came to it. For now, he needed to get inside the building without being stopped.

With a deep breath, he made a beeline toward the door.

"Hey," a voice called from behind. Rowan knew better than to stop. He kept his chin tucked to his chest and casually waved without looking back. "Jerk-off."

Rowan had been called many names over the years. Jerk-off fell low on the list of offensive ones. So low, in fact, he cracked a smile when he probably should have been offended. He couldn't help it. He'd managed to slip in through the backdoor without being stopped.

"Where the hell do you think you're going?" Mr. Clean asked from somewhere behind Rowan.

Could he ignore this one?

~

WAITING WAS THE WORST. Tara had very little patience on a good day. The stakes were so high on this she could reach the top of Mount Everest if she stood on them. She'd lost visual contact with Rowan after he rounded the back of the building. It wasn't difficult to guess what he was up to. Going in through the back was a smart idea. She had to give it to him. The van had presented itself at an opportune time.

This was a good thing. So, why did her pulse race and her heart pound the inside of her ribcage?

The obvious answer was the fact this was risky. No one knew him, though. He had the upper hand. All he had to do was go inside and check on her mom. Then what? It wasn't like Tara could snatch her mom from rehab, take her to a safehouse.

Witness protection sounded like a good idea right now. Except that she had no idea who the Lieutenant was or who worked for him. When Xander first talked about the Lieutenant, she thought he was talking about someone from work, a superior officer. It had taken her a while to figure out the Lieutenant was a nickname.

Would the law know who the Lieutenant was? Wouldn't there be some kind of organized crime division she could speak to?

Not now that she was a cop killer. The flashbacks of Xander finding her and then chasing her deeper into the forest while she ran at lightning speed. The only reason she'd been able to gain the upper hand was because he'd torn a ligament in his knee. Otherwise, there would have been no way she could outrun him. He was a solid runner. Seeing him limp as he came at her gave her the idea to run in the first place. Then, the self defense lessons had paid off. They'd taught her to run in a zigzag through trees if there was a possible shooter. They'd taught her to use an opponent's body weight against them, like she had when Xander had jumped on top of her from the evergreen he'd been hiding inside.

Tara had lost her way in the forest. Whereas he must have known where she would end up, given the path they were on. He must have run down the mountain, cutting through evergreens, while she'd taken the path.

One moment, she was making progress and starting to feel like she might actually get out of the forest alive. The next, his heavy body was on top of hers and she was eating dirt. His strong hands were around her neck, choking her. Tara managed to flip over, determined to fight back. She might have been able to outrun him but Xander had more hand and arm strength.

Somehow, she'd managed to buck him off. He'd grunted and then mumbled something about pain in his knee. She'd been able to stomp on his ankle before she took off running again.

Tree branches slapped her face as she'd bolted through the evergreens. But she couldn't care about anything other than getting away from the monster she'd once shared a bed with. Shame filled her at the thought he'd slipped right by her radar. She should have known better.

By some miracle, Xander didn't stay down for long. This time, he drew his gun and walked through the trees. He'd grown up in this forest. She should have remembered that fact, but there'd been no time to think, only act.

Tara had located the only weapon she could find, a rock with an edge almost as sharp as a knife. Twigs had snapped, alerting her to his presence or he would have gotten the best of her twice. Even with all the defense lessons she'd had, he was a step ahead. The twig had given him away, so she'd decided right then and there she was done running. She palmed the rock and waited.

Now, she involuntarily shivered at the thought she'd taken someone's life. Xander deserved to be brought to justice, not murdered.

Tears welled in her eyes thinking about it. She had barely had a chance to catch her breath since it happened. Since she left Xander lying on the ground bleeding. The image would haunt her for the rest of her life. All the training in the world couldn't prepare her for taking someone's life. Despite a rough start in life, she didn't have killer instincts. She didn't get any satisfaction out of his death, no peace of mind. In fact, she would most likely never rest easy again.

Being near Rowan brought on a feeling of calm. With him, the world righted itself and she could breathe without feeling like the air had been sucked out of the room. Even in the cab of the truck right now, it hurt to do something as simple as take in air.

The kiss they'd shared had hinted of so much more than fire and chemistry. It touched her in a place she'd locked away a long time ago in order to protect herself. The thing about self-defense lessons was they only helped with physical confrontations. There was no way to shield her heart without tucking her feelings down deep and building high walls to keep everyone out.

Did she keep Grace and Rudy out too?

In all honesty, the answer was probably yes. They'd come the closest to breaking through. She was devoted to Rudy's memory and to staying by Grace's side no matter the personal cost. But she could only go so far when it came to risking her heart.

A little voice in the back of her mind picked that moment to point out she had most likely gotten into relationship after relationship with men she could never truly love. The realization struck like a sucker punch.

Another gut punch came in the form of everything she was going to give up if she had to leave town. Her business, for one. She'd built it from the ground up and it was a huge source of pride. The thought of walking away from it felt like a slap in the face. A growing part of her wanted to dig her heels in and fight for real justice.

But it would mean giving up everything familiar once again. How many times had she been ripped out of one environment to be dropped into the next? Too many. She'd lost count. It wasn't like the new place ended up being some great improvement either. The situation generally went downhill in a heartbeat. All the more reason she loved Grace and Rudy. They'd been patient when she'd shown up almost feral by civilized standards. There'd been too many times she'd ended up locked in a closet and denied food for her to instantly trust anyone.

Could she disappear and leave Grace? Could she live a quiet life somewhere no one would ever look for her? Where would she go? Out of the country? Make a fresh start in Canada? Mexico? Europe?

The thought of never being able to contact Grace again, especially when her mom needed Tara the most was enough to bring on a steady stream of tears along with a wave of crippling anxiety. Tucking her tail between her legs and running went against everything she believed in, so she wouldn't. Feelings were just that...feelings. They weren't rational.

Tara made her own decisions. Going back to the witness protection idea, the Lieutenant would most likely ruin the business she would be leaving behind, even if she left it in good hands with her second in command. He would definitely go after her family, which was only Grace. Her mom was the only person Tara considered family. She'd lost track of her biological parents years ago and never looked back. She didn't try to hire a detective or ask Xander to do a little digging around. No one had tried to contact her either.

Risking anything happening to Grace wasn't something she could do. With her mom in rehab, could Tara go into protective custody and take Grace along with her?

Then, there was the whole situation with Xander. Her DNA was all over him. The man had jumped her, injured her. The Lieutenant had connections that could help taint the crime scene and the scenario under which Xander had died. He would most likely be hailed a hero, while she was vilified. On paper, why would anyone believe her side of the story? A cop with a spotless record would be looked at with far more regard than someone who'd been in and out of the system. Would folks care that she'd cleaned up her life? Would they care she'd contributed to society with jobs?

It was true that she wasn't the friendliest person, which was exactly the reason she'd started a business involving animals. They were so much easier than humans. Human interaction wasn't her biggest asset. Folks left her alone to work her magic. Taking care of animals gave her so much more satisfaction than dealing with people—people confused the hell out of her most of the time.

Tara studied the exact spot where Rowan had disappeared a while ago. What was taking so long?

She issued a sharp sigh. It might be a good idea to get out and stretch her legs for a minute. Mid-reach for the door, she stopped herself. No. Getting out of the truck would be the exact moment Rowan would come running out the front door needing her help.

Instead, she tapped on the steering wheel and waited. She almost wished she'd taken his cell phone. Maybe they could stop off once she knew her mom was alright and being well cared for in order to buy a burner phone. Something she could throw away when this was over and her cell was recovered.

Tara's mind drifted to Rowan. He'd said he had unlimited funds. Could she allow him to step in and have her mom transferred? Or would that draw unwanted attention to him? To her mom?

Her mom was receiving excellent care here as best as Tara could tell. The rehab center was highly rated and reviewed. The doctors, nurses, and therapists seemed to care about each patient. Security was solid here. Then again, they were testing it out right now. If Rowan doesn't get stopped, Tara should probably be concerned.

Maybe she should have just made a call to check on her mom even though she had no idea how far the Lieutenant's reach might be. He might have someone on the inside keeping watch over her mom to see if Tara showed her face. It dawned on her that would be the easiest way for him to get to her.

More of that panic caused her heart to jackhammer the inside of her ribs. Where was Rowan?

11

When in doubt, keep walking. The motto had always worked for Rowan. He'd managed to get inside the backdoor of the rehab facility. He'd managed to avoid making eye contact with Mr. Clean. And now, he used the motto to figure out where in hell's name he was in the building he'd never once set foot in before now.

A set of stairs sat to the right up ahead. He'd made it out of the back and into the main hallway. Don't ask how because he couldn't say after walking through a labyrinth. He'd taken door number three on his left and ended up here. At least he wasn't stuck at the long counter at the front door trying to convince the desk worker to allow him past the proverbial gates.

All he had to do now was find Room 222. Should be easy enough. The trick was not being stopped by one of the nurses or orderlies on the floor.

Ballcap down, chin to chest, he blocked as much of his face as possible by making it difficult to walk in between him and the wall on one side. The bouquet hid his face from the opposite direction. No one had stopped him so far, despite being called out by the driver and Mr. Clean.

Rowan had no idea how he'd escaped Mr. Clean. The only explanation was the driver must have come in right after Rowan, distracting the muscled man with questions or a delivery. Mumbling the word *bathroom* after Mr. Clean shouted at Rowan must have worked. He'd walked the hall half expecting to be jerked backward by the collar of his shirt at any moment. Risking a glance back might have invited trouble, so Rowan hadn't dared. Looking like he knew what he was doing had kept him out of plenty of entanglements in the past. Thankfully, this situation had proved no different.

Between the wheelchairs and folks trying to walk on crutches throughout the hallways, the place was lively. He figured it made it easier for him to blend in even though the hall was a sea of hospital-issued clothing and scrubs.

Taking a right at the last minute to jog up the stairs, he nearly crashed into a guy in scrubs who was rushing down.

"Excuse me," Rowan said, keeping his head down. He bit back a curse.

"My fault," the orderly said. "Sorry about the water on your shirt."

Damn. The guy was noticing details about Rowan. He wanted to remain as anonymous as possible, which meant drawing as little attention as he could get away with.

"No problem," Rowan said. *Keep climbing.*

The orderly didn't move. "Hey, can I help you with something? There aren't supposed to be any delivery people—"

"Sandy buzzed me in," he said as he continued to climb the curved staircase. Getting in was hard enough. What was it going to be like when he had to get out? Being caught by security didn't exactly jive with his incognito approach.

"Who?" The man was persistent.

Rowan rounded the stairwell, finally out of sight. He didn't stop but he did keep going past the second floor just in case Orderly followed.

When the coast was clear, Rowan doubled back, not thrilled someone could identify him in court later if all of this blew up in his and Tara's faces.

Room 222 was easy enough to find. It was the second room to the right of the stairwell. The door was cracked open so he slipped inside unnoticed. The light was off so he left it that way. A short entryway was the only thing between him and Grace Goodman.

The bathroom door to his right was closed and the light was on inside. He heard shuffling noises and then a toilet flush. Rather than stand at the door, he took the couple of steps deeper inside the room with one bed.

A clunk sounded from the bathroom along with a squeal.

"Help," a frail voice he imagined must belong to Grace said.

"Coming in," he said, setting down the vase on the side table next to the bed before making a beeline toward the door.

"Please," came the strained voice. His heart went out to her. She sounded desperate and vulnerable.

"I'm coming inside," he said. After a quick tap on the door, he opened it and rushed to the older woman who was curled up on her side on the bathroom floor. The water was still running and the sink was filling up, about to overflow. "I'm right here."

Grace turned to look at him—eyes wide—and gasped.

An object struck the back of his head. Then a second strike.

"Did you really think you could get away with this?" a male voice said.

Rowan tried to spin around to get a look at his attacker, but nausea slammed into him like a rogue wave. The room started to spin and his eyes lost focus before everything went dark.

With great effort, Rowan pushed through to the darkness to find he was slumped over in a wheelchair. His first thought was Tara. Had the bastards gotten to her too? No. He reasoned the men were here in Grace's room, where they'd expected Tara to show up.

The rehab facility had good security, but it wasn't impenetrable. He'd made it into the building and up to Grace's room without being questioned too hard. He squinted his eyes open to see a blanket had been thrown over his lap. He still had on his street clothes but he'd been moved into Grace's room and out of the bathroom.

The fact someone got the drop on him made his hands fist. He forced them to relax but he would be ready, should the jerk with the voice decide to get close enough for Rowan to attack. Before he made a move, he needed to get the lay of the land. How many jerks were there? Two? Three?

There was one inside the hospital, who was here in the room with them. Were there others waiting outside? In the parking lot? He forced his hands to relax on his thighs so he didn't give away the fact he was conscious. Right now, he had the element of surprise on his side.

Making a commotion while still in the room would get him out of a sticky situation, but what about Tara in the parking lot? Had she seen them first? Driven away? Or was she bound and gagged in the back of a van or truck or SUV?

His muscles chorded just thinking about her being taken hostage. Killing her while out in the open would be a mistake. If she was down in the parking lot, she was most likely still alive.

Of course, everything was a guess at this point. All the more reason to stay calm and fight the urge to deck the bastard who'd jumped him a few minutes ago.

Rowan couldn't get a good visual on Grace. At this point, he was happy to be alive. Then again, a dead person would draw a heap of unwanted attention. Anyone who did a little digging into the situation would be able to link Grace to Tara, which, in turn, would connect them to the cop who was killed. It would be too big of a mess to clean up easily.

Their best bet would be to set up a fake suicide to get rid of Tara. They could have her hang herself in her home with a note of apology about killing the cop. A murder-suicide would neatly tie up any witnesses.

Grace seemed out of it. She was most likely on medication that would make anything she said suspect. He had no idea if Grace knew her own name or remembered Tara while so heavily medicated. A head injury was nothing to play around with. It had to be taken seriously. The one thing he was certain of was that she could follow instructions. The Voice had to have given her orders. Had he seen Rowan walking down the hallway and then ducked into the room? Was the Voice there to assess the situation? Did they find Xander's body? Did Rowan just interrupt an abduction in process? If so, someone had to be down in the parking lot watching.

Keeping his body in the slumped position, Rowan tried to glance around without giving himself away.

The sounds of feet shuffling behind him was followed by

a shove forward. Limp, he let his head roll forward. Long fingers gripped his skull and forced his head to one side.

"You're going to hurt the ragdoll," Grace warned with a tsk-tsk quality to her voice. She sounded almost like a little girl scolding one of her dolls.

"You keep quiet like we said and no one will come back to hurt you," Voice said.

Every sound was like someone took a hammer to the back of Rowen's skull. He felt a cool liquid dripping down the back of his neck and wondered how severe of a blow he'd taken.

"I don't like getting hurt," Grace said. He imagined her face was pinched now. He thought about the fact she was the only family Tara had left. His chest squeezed. A growing part of him wanted to find a way to rectify the situation. Tara didn't deserve the horrific childhood she'd endured. She didn't deserve to be bounced around in the system. And she sure as hell didn't deserve to have the only family she knew ripped from her.

Tara was facing serious charges when it came to killing a cop. If she was right, no one would believe she'd murdered a man and then fled the scene in self-defense. Most folks would immediately call 911. It was the logical action. But people who'd endured abusive pasts and relationships didn't always do what society deemed as upstanding in these events. He'd read various accounts in the news over the years.

"We're going for a ride," Voice said as he shoved the wheelchair forward again. "Open the door, Grace." Voice was a lot sterner this time.

Could Grace walk?

It took every ounce of willpower inside Rowan not to swing around and sucker punch Voice. Making a move, before he knew the threat he faced, could be a critical mistake. One that could cost Grace her life, not to mention his own. Where would Tara end up if he wasn't around to help her? Her circumstances were dire but she had help. If anything happened to him, she had no one. Grace was in no condition to help and there was no way Tara would leave her mom. Not while she needed her.

After this visit, he understood Tara's position all too well. It took a huge heart for a person to risk their own safety, not to mention life, in order to be there for someone else. The sacrifice Tara was making to be around for Grace was humbling. Tara had integrity in buckets. And yet the odds she would come out of this unscathed were slim to none. They dropped to zero without help. He wanted to be the one to give her a hand up more than he wanted to breathe. She deserved a break.

Hell, he used to believe he was the unluckiest person on earth. It wasn't until meeting Tara that he was beginning to see just how fortunate he was. Wasn't that how it worked? It took watching someone truly get the short end of the stick to realize his life wasn't so bad, which said a lot considering his mother was in jail.

He'd come to Colorado to clear his mind. It had taken a random meeting in a forest for him to come to the understanding he didn't need space. He needed to visit his mother and give her a chance to tell her side of the story.

There was only one problem. If Voice had his way, Rowan wouldn't live long enough to return to Texas. As he was being wheeled out the door and down the hallway, it occurred to him Voice must be wearing scrubs. Going in, Rowan hadn't wanted to draw attention. This time would be different. He needed to bide his time, wait for the hallway to be full of people, and then make a move.

Soon. Very soon.

~

The duct tape over Tara's mouth prevented her from shouting to warn Rowan when he stepped out of the building and into the sun. *If he made it out alive.* She'd been caught off guard when she stepped out for a second to stretch her legs. She'd checked her mirrors first, saw no one. The men who grabbed her were pros, but she should have expected as much.

Money laundering was only one of their crimes. She'd heard whispers of this group having their hands in weapons and human trafficking. The last one hit her even harder than the others.

Could she still figure out a way to warn Rowan?

If he made it out alive, he would come back to an empty truck. She'd managed to shove the key inside her front pocket without being caught so at least she still had that. She had no idea why no one had checked her pockets for a phone. Everything had happened so fast. The key had already been in her fingers as she toyed with it.

Hands tied behind her back made movement next to impossible, as she sat on the floor in the second row of the SUV. The pair of men who'd gotten to her waited for the driver. Part of her wished Rowan would run far away.

By now, Xander's body would have likely been found. A search would have occurred. Or his location would have been given away by his cell phone. Why hadn't she thought to take it with her and toss it onto a moving vehicle to throw folks off and buy more time?

You're not a criminal, a voice in the back of her mind pointed out. It was true, though. Only a criminal would have thought through all the details of their crime or known exactly what to do to divert attention or make it nearly impossible to find Xander's body in the heat of the moment. The worst crimes she'd committed in her youth were truancy and shoplifting. She'd lied too, but that was more like making up stories of how she wished her life would be rather than the reality of what it had been.

Since the pair of men, both dressed in scrubs, were still here, she assumed a third and possibly even more were inside. She also guessed no one had gotten to Rowan yet or they would be on the road.

When it came to being abducted, Tara knew her best chance of survival was to figure out a way to break free now. If these bastards managed to take her to another location, she would most definitely die.

Where was Rowan?

Was it possible he'd figured out someone was on the inside? Waiting? Or had this group just arrived?

Not knowing what was going on inside the building was the worst.

And then another dark thought struck. Had they led these bastards straight to Grace's door?

12

The hallway was almost empty. Considering Rowan was in a wheelchair, he would have to be taken downstairs via the elevator. There was a good chance someone else would be in the elevator. The building had been buzzing with activity on his way in. Would someone intervene? Stop them? There had to be some kind of protocol for taking patients outside. A check-out process of sorts.

Then again, it was just his luck that everyone would be inside rooms and the halls would be quiet when he needed them to be just the opposite. Damn bad luck.

Patience wins wars. He repeated the mantra until he almost believed it.

Voice whistled as he pushed the chair. Rowan wished for a mirror on the wall or something that could give him a general description of the man. Someone getting the drop on him sat heavy in his gut.

Where did this leave Tara? Were there more people outside? Was she still in the parking lot?

Rowan's cell was still inside his pocket, a small but important miracle.

As they neared the elevator, the sound of glass breaking down the hall was followed by the screech of fire sirens. Lights flashed. Voice cursed. He took a few seconds to assess and then doubled back toward Grace's room to a throng of patients filling the hall.

This was Rowan's moment. He hopped to his feet and then moved behind a couple of folks who were standing side-by-side, looking around like they were trying to figure out what was going on.

Voice was shy of six feet tall but thick. He had on scrubs and a surgical mask, like was common among workers in medical facilities. Rowan wished he thought of wearing one to hide his face.

All he could see clearly was Voice had dark eyes and curly dark hair that was fairly short. The guy had a tattoo of a snake winding down a dagger on his left arm. His skin was olive-colored and it looked like he spent a fair amount of time in the sun.

The man was heading toward Grace's room. Snatching her would be a sure way to draw Tara out into the open if they didn't have her already. Voice gripped his cell phone. Was he warning a team downstairs?

"Everyone stay calm," Voice said with authority as he scanned faces, no doubt searching for Rowan who was hidden in a group. He was selling the line. "Step back against the wall."

Voice put his cell to his ear as he turned to face the opposite direction, no doubt about to check in with whoever else was here. Rowan knew in an instant that he couldn't allow that to happen. So he sprung from behind the small group, sprinted, and then dove toward Voice's back.

As he made contact, the cell flew from Voice's grip before banging hard onto the tile floor. Voice launched forward, face-planting on the hard tile. They skidded with Rowan on Voice's back.

The second he could, Rowan hopped to his feet and made a run for the phone. He had to get to Tara. Having the cell would definitely help not only figure out who was behind all this but possibly locate the others. At the very least, it was evidence. The more evidence they had, the better Tara's case would be.

Without a minute to lose, Rowan scooped up the phone and darted toward the stairwell. Grace's door was closed as he ran past. Good for her. She must have been the one to set off the alarm. How? He had no idea but he fully intended to hug her once this was all over. Her mind was clear enough to know danger when it walked into her room and forced her to fake a fall in the bathroom.

Good. They could double back later and get her the help she needed. He was all in at this point, especially after getting to know Tara and witnessing Grace's resolve. Even now, after everything she'd been through, something inside the older woman wanted to protect Tara.

Every muscle in his body chorded at the thought someone had to have either been waiting for them to show or followed them here to the rehab center. Tara didn't have a cell, so no one could have been able to trace her movements. They'd been careful on the drive over. It was possible they'd linked Rowan to Tara.

He scrambled down the stairs and retraced his steps until he was outside and behind the building again. No one shouted at him this time with the fire alarm screeching in the background. No one bothered with him at all as orderlies scrambled to keep folks lined up against the wall as they figured out what to do next.

Running full throttle around the back of the building probably wasn't a good idea. One man was already on the inside. Rowan didn't figure the guy was acting alone. He would have a driver at the very least and possibly another accomplice on the outside. Reason said there most likely wouldn't be more than three in total for this operation, but that was only a guess on his part. The men would be looking for Tara and had most likely been caught off guard when Rowan had shown up. There was no way for them to know his identity, so he doubted anyone would come looking for him.

If they had Tara, that was a whole different story altogether. Anger welled up inside him at the thought. He clenched his back teeth so hard he thought they might crack. They would have taken her from his truck and, therefore, most likely taken a picture of his license plate. If this crime ring had the right connections, they'd be able to run his plates and figure out who he was that way. Did he need to alert the ranch to a possible threat?

Even if they ran his Texas plates, he could be someone Tara used for a ride or tricked into going inside. There was no reason to believe the two knew each other or were personally connected in any way. Given their backgrounds, it didn't make sense they would have any type of relationship, be it personal or professional.

Back against the brick wall, Rowan eased toward the corner. He glanced across the parking lot but his truck was parked too far away to get a visual. Besides, he'd told Tara to stay down low. If she was doing just that, he wouldn't be able to see her until he was right on top of the truck. Could this situation get any worse?

The answer to his question came a second later when it felt like a vise gripped his arm. The next thing he knew, his hand was being jerked behind his back and shoved in between his shoulder blades. Cold metal poked him underneath his shirt in between his ribs. The barrel was distinct. The weapon was a gun.

"Try running from me again," Voice said.

Rowan bit back a curse.

"Where are we going?" he asked the bastard.

"Don't worry about it," Voice said.

Making a move before he knew what was going on with Tara wasn't a good idea. *Patience.*

Frustration nipped at Rowan's heels as they walked across the chaotic parking lot. The guy wouldn't shoot unless his hand was forced. Not with all these people around. He might, however, get nervous enough to twitch on his trigger finger. If the safety was off, Rowan would have a hole in his torso. Since he wasn't trying to become Swiss cheese, he didn't fight against what was happening to him. The other issue was Tara. He had no idea what was going on with her. At least Grace was safe for the time being.

With his truck now in sight, his hopes of her getting away in time diminished in front of his eyes. More of that frustration seethed. These bastards had her. Would they take both of them to the same place? Would they keep them apart? Rowan didn't have a criminal bone in his body but common sense said these jerks would keep the two separated.

Unless…

It was possible they only had one vehicle, in which case there would be no choice but to be together. Did he dare hope?

As they neared the truck, his heart sank. She wasn't

there, which wasn't totally unexpected, but seeing the reality of it caused a knot to form in the center of his chest. Breathing was hard. He swallowed for lack of anything better to do. With the gun jammed into his ribcage, he didn't dare make a move. Not to mention the fact an innocent person could end up hurt or killed by shrapnel.

"Open the door," Voice demanded.

"I can't unless it's unlocked," Rowan said. "I don't have the key."

Voice bit out a curse. He shoved Rowan against the truck. "Give me my cell."

It seemed the Lieutenant, or whoever was behind this, wanted to keep Rowan and Tara separated. He was smart to do it that way. Smarter than Rowan wanted him to be.

Then again, the man headed up a successful crime ring. He didn't rise to the top by leaving things to chance or making mistakes.

Chest against the hood of his truck, Rowan could easily use his free hand to push off giving him the extra force he needed to ram into Voice. A headbutt would do the trick. Rowan had learned to fight growing up with his siblings and cousins. There'd been wrestling matches and boxing fights on a regular basis as a kid growing up on the ranch. He'd taken his fair share of punches, kicks, and objects being chucked at him. Rowan was no stranger to a fight.

Time had come to test his skills against this bastard.

TARA MANAGED to slip her bound hands underneath her feet, finagling until they were in front of her rather than behind her back. Now that she had the use of both, she could ease the duct tape off her mouth. A fire alarm inside the rehab center had caused the jerks in the SUV to exit the vehicle so they could check it out. For her, it was now or never.

Impatience edged as her hands shook. She yanked off the tape. Her lips burned and it felt like the worst wax she'd ever experienced, but she could breathe better and that was a good start. Next, she bit a nodule on the tape binding her wrists together. From there, it was easy to rip off the bindings. Once her hands were free, she was able to easily remove her ankles from bondage.

The SUV was still running. The men were out of sight. She climbed on top of the center console before claiming the driver's seat. Not twenty feet in front of her, the bastards who'd snatched her from the truck stood. The SUV was parked down the road and out of view of the rehab center, which was the reason her and Rowan had missed them. The guys stood there, hands on their hips, staring toward the facility.

Everything was happening so fast, it hardly felt real. Yet, here she was, about to ram two men with a vehicle. She wished she could find a way to get ahold of Rowan to see what happened to him. The fire alarm made her feel like maybe there was a chance he'd gotten out of the rehab facility alive. Would he think of taking Grace with him? If anything happened to her mom, Tara would never forgive herself. In that case, she might as well go to jail for the rest of her life because nothing else would matter. Rowan came to mind. He was beginning to feel like family but not in a brotherly or fatherly way.

Making a move now without knowing what was going on with Rowan or Grace was risky but she couldn't let these bastards stand there untouched. They would turn back to the SUV in a matter of minutes, and then what?

Moving the seat up while maintaining a low profile, Tara took a deep breath. *On the count of three.*

One.

Two.

Three.

Tara mashed the gas, pressing the pedal down as far as it would go. The tires spun, searching for purchase. They caught and the SUV jerked forward.

The roar of the engine caught the attention of bastards number one and two. They turned to face her as the SUV barreled toward them. Eyes wide, One dove into Two, knocking his associate out of the way in the nick of time. A bump said One took a small hit. A shouted curse said he would live.

The surprising fact about both men was they looked exactly like someone she could stand next to in line at a coffee shop and not think twice. They were on the tall side —not nearly as tall as Rowan, but few were—and looked to be in their mid- to late-twenties. They were average looking. They wore regular clothes of jeans and a button-down. Nothing spectacular or that screamed *criminal,* which was probably the reason they were successful.

Tara navigated the SUV toward the parking lot, praying like everything that Rowan was not only okay but somewhere she could find him. She jumped a curb and drove over a small patch of grass as cars jammed the entrance and exit to the lot, making entry impossible by any other means.

The truck was parked at the back of the lot. She immediately saw Rowan and a man in scrubs who was shorter and thick. Thick arms. Thick legs. Thick had on a surgical mask and scrubs but she would bet money he didn't work at the rehab center. *Grace.*

Tara prayed her mom was unharmed. She had to shove

the thought aside for now as she aimed toward the truck and pressed the gas pedal harder.

Rowan was shoved up against his vehicle with Thick standing a little too close behind him. She flashed high beams at the men, hoping Rowan could see her in the driver's seat. It was getting late in the afternoon and the sun was retreating.

Thick performed a double take, realized she was behind the wheel at the same time as Rowan. Rowan, however, made the first move. He spun around, knocking a weapon that looked like a gun out of Thick's hand. A second later, Rowan threw a punch that connected with Thick's jaw, causing his head to snap to the right.

Tara slammed on the brake as she cut the wheel to bring the passenger door near Rowan. He performed a back-wheel kick that caused Thick to stumble backward, creating enough distance for Rowan to bolt toward the passenger side.

She put the gearshift in Park to unlock the doors. Rowan jumped inside the vehicle as Thick hopped to his feet and gaited toward them. Turning the wheel to aim directly at him, she put the gearshift in Drive and mashed the gas pedal again.

Thick's eyes practically bulged out of his head when he saw how serious she was about running him over if he didn't get out of her way. He jumped left, giving her a wide berth as she flew over the nearest curb and onto the closest street.

"I'm sorry," she said to Rowan as he scooted toward her.

"Don't be," he reassured. "Do you want me to drive?"

"Yes," she admitted, heart threatening to tenderize her ribcage.

"I'll slide in behind you," he said. "Keep your foot on the gas and eyes on the road, and we'll be fine."

The rehab center became smaller and smaller in the rearview. "They'll hurt her."

"I know," he said as he moved behind her, his powerful thighs wrapped around her.

She stopped at a red light in moderate traffic.

"Ready?" he asked.

She slipped the gearshift into Park momentarily as they made the trade. And then she climbed over the console to the passenger side where she clicked her seatbelt on.

"Any idea who this vehicle belongs to?" Rowan asked as he put the gearshift in Drive and navigated around traffic after the light turned green.

Tara leaned her head against the rest and rubbed her temples. "We lost all your supplies. Everything is in your truck."

"They'll pillage through my belongings," he said on a sharp sigh.

Tara reached inside her pocket and pulled out the key. "Not without this, they won't."

"You have the key?" he asked with the first real sound of hope in his voice.

"I managed to slip it inside my pocket after those two men surprised me," she said. "Those were some impressive moves back there, by the way."

"Growing up with a boatload of brothers and cousins will do that to a person," he said. "Do you know who they are?"

"Never seen them before in my life," she admitted. "I didn't think the Lieutenant would come himself, though."

"Wishful thinking on my part," he said. "But I had to ask."

"To be honest, I have no idea who the Lieutenant is," she said. "I've never met him personally. He threatened me once over the phone but I didn't recognize his voice. Did you ever talk into a fan when you were a kid?"

"Yes," he said.

"His voice sounded kind of like that," she explained.

"I thought he was most likely your ex's brother," he admitted.

"I don't know what to think anymore," she said on a sharp sigh.

"Did those two say anything that might give us a clue?"

"We're riding in the only clue I have," she said, glancing around before looking onto the glovebox. She opened it. "There should be an insurance card or registration somewhere in here, right?"

Rowan nodded as he cracked a smile. "I could see these men getting cocky. Using this vehicle for criminal activity and then thinking they're too good to get caught so why take the insurance card out."

Tara held up a piece of paper. "We might have just found our first real lead."

13

"That doesn't look like insurance papers," Rowan said, catching the bright yellow out of the corner of his eye.

"Nope," Tara agreed. "This is from his last oil change." She scanned the top of the highlighted yellow page, muttering as she read. "Here it is. Marcus Payne."

"Payne?" Rowan said.

"Could be a fake name," Tara reasoned.

"My first thought exactly," he agreed. "But that doesn't necessarily mean anything. His last name could actually be Payne."

"Stranger things have happened," she said. Then gasped. "Oh, hold on. I think I might know who this is. At least, I know I've heard Xander mention the name in the past. I thought he was talking in some kind of code when he mentioned Payne. He'd say something like, 'Payne did something,' and I thought he was trying to hide the real name in case I was listening to his conversation."

"At the very least, Payne is this guy's street name," he reasoned.

"Wouldn't he need some form of identification to pull this name off at places like Oil Change Quick?" she asked.

"Career criminals have their ways," he pointed out. "If this organization is as powerful as I think it is, it wouldn't take much to have a convincing identity created along with associated papers."

"How do I get myself out of this, Rowan?" The momentary defeat in her voice practically gutted him.

"We keep gathering evidence to support our side of the story, for one."

"I still don't know who the Lieutenant is and I can only hide out for so long," she countered. "They've found my mom, so it's only a matter of time before they come back to the rehab center."

"Once we know we're out of the woods here, I'll make arrangements for her to be taken to a secure location," Rowan said. "With your permission, of course."

"I wouldn't know how to thank you," she said. "That being said, please do whatever you can to keep her safe and I'll find a way."

"Your mom saved my life back there," he said. "She risked herself to help me get away. I owe her."

Tara reached over and touched his arm. The now-familiar electrical impulse vibrated up his arm and sent warmth spiraling through him. He could get used to the feeling. Should he, though?

"That's just how she's made," Tara said with a tenderness in her voice now. "Believe me when I say a lesser person would have given up on me when I showed up at her and Rudy's doorstep. I was drenched with rain. The skies opened up that day with a shower like none I've ever seen. I took it as an omen, so I immediately slipped out my new bedroom window after being left alone for five minutes. I became a regular Houdini in those years."

"You were a survivor," he said. "Still are."

A small smile toyed with her lips at the compliment.

"The storm got worse and I had no idea where I was," she said. "My cell had been taken away, so I had no way to reach out to anyone. I had no money. Rudy and Grace hopped in their minivan and searched until they found me sitting on a street corner. Soaked. I didn't want to go to yet another home that would end up hurting me. I was done."

"Understandable," he reassured. "You'd been through more than any young person should have to endure."

"They were...*are* angels," she said, staring out the passenger side window. "I couldn't live with myself if anything happened to..."

"We'll get Grace to safety," he promised when she couldn't finish the sentence. "You have my word."

In fact, he needed to pull over so he could make the call soon.

"I need a good spot," he said, thinking out loud, as he scanned the area.

"How about we park behind that building," she said, pointing to the big box store coming up on their left.

"Good idea," he said, navigating to the turn lane. The roads in this town were two-lane and narrow. The parking lot of the store buzzed like they were giving everything away. He glanced at the clock. The sun was down, and his stomach reminded him they hadn't eaten in a long while. Fronting the parking lot was a fast-food burger chain. There was a gas station owned by the big box store beside it. "Are you hungry?"

"I should eat," she said. It was understandable that she

might not feel hungry after the adrenaline rush. But she was right. She needed to get something in her stomach.

He pulled into the drive-through and got in line behind half a dozen vehicles. This necessary stop left them exposed because the lane was closed off. In an SUV, he could pop the curb if need be but there was a trash system along with a brick wall for part of it that he wouldn't be able to get around. In essence, they'd be locked in for a period of time. Rowan didn't like it but they needed food and this was the most convenient option at this point.

Time to suck it up, buttercup.

After placing their orders of burgers, fries, and drinks, he tapped his finger on the steering wheel while waiting for the line to move.

"I have the cell of one of those bastards," he finally said as they inched forward. Progress was slow but there was a steady rhythm. He fished in his pocket and produced it. "Want to play around with it and see if you can get anything?"

He held it out on the flat of his palm.

Tara took the offering and tapped the screen. "It needs facial recognition or a passcode."

"I figured as much," he said. "Throw some numbers in and see what happens."

She did as he pulled around to the spot where they were the most hemmed in. He also realized it would be more difficult to see them here. If there was a silver lining, that had to be it.

"I'm not getting anything," she said after tinkering. She set the phone down in the cup holder on the console before pinching the bridge of her nose. She exhaled a slow breath. "I killed someone, Rowan. How will I ever live with that? How can I eat knowing Xander will never…"

Her bringing up the subject made him realize there should be a news report by now if the body was found. A missing cop would make headlines. At the very least, his employer should have noticed. "Take my phone and search for any news of a local cop's death."

Tara did after he unlocked it with facial recognition.

She tapped the screen and then studied it as he moved forward another space.

"This is strange," she said, not looking up. Her forehead wrinkled in concern. "There's nothing about Xander."

"It's possible he hasn't been recovered yet," he reasoned.

"Maybe we should go back up to the spot," she stated with the first sign of what sounded like hope since this ordeal began. "To check and see what activity there's been."

"It's possible the chief doesn't want bad publicity until he knows what happened and or has someone behind bars," Rowan said. "He might sit on the news as long as he can."

She shook her head. "I doubt it. I'm sure he'd be asking for leads if Xander's body was found." An involuntary shiver rocked her as her voice cracked on the last words.

"Okay," he said, needing to chew on this one. Speaking of which, he pulled up to the window, paid, and then set the bag on the console as Tara took the drinks.

Exiting the drive-through, he surveyed the area. He wasn't sure what he was looking for exactly. Someone paying too close attention to their surroundings maybe. The bastards from the rehab center had no transportation. At least, not at the moment. Even if they ordered a car on one of those apps, it would take time for it to arrive and he highly doubted they'd be thinking about going to one of these big box stores.

On the other hand, the perps knew exactly what they were looking for since Rowan was driving a vehicle that belonged to them and they could trace the phone he took. Unless, of course, the feature had been blocked, which would make sense since they wouldn't want their location to be tracked.

As he crossed the parking lot heading toward the back of the building, a police SUV parked toward the left caught his eye. It was dark outside at this point, making it easier to see the officer inside. The cab was lit by the computer screen. The vehicle's headlights were dimmed.

For some strange reason, Rowan got a bad feeling. Maybe it was because they were running from the cops, or maybe it was because Tara had killed one of their own, but he couldn't shake it.

"Do you mind sinking down in the seat?" he asked her. "I don't like the cop sitting over there."

"Okay," she said as she did. "Is he watching?"

"He's staring at his screen right now," he informed. "It's probably nothing but me being paranoid."

"Better safe than sorry," she said.

He wondered if he could ever make her feel safe again.

The cop's headlights flipped on. And then, his red and blue strobe lights came to life.

Rowan bit back a curse as the vehicle pulled up behind them, and then put on his siren.

∽

"The second I tell you, you slip out of the passenger seat and out of the vehicle." Rowan's voice was a study in calm whereas Tara was freaking out. The thought of everything crashing down around her while her mom paid the price sucked the air out of her lungs. The Lieutenant had expressly spelled out what he would do to Grace Goodman if Tara didn't comply.

"Tell me when," she said, hearing and hating the shakiness in her own voice as Rowan pulled beside a row of cars.

"Stay low, okay?"

"I'm not budging until you tell me to," she reassured as her pulse jacked up a few more notches.

Rowan kept his gaze focused on the officer behind them. He brought his hand up then tapped the interior light above the console, keeping his hands high where they could be seen at all times. "Go now."

She slipped out of the passenger seat, keeping a low profile. She closed the door as softly as she could before sliding in between two vehicles. The cart return was two cars down. Could she grab a cart and then pretend to be heading into the store to shop?

What was the plan?

Risking a glance back would be a mistake, so she didn't no matter how strong the pull became. Rowan knew what he was doing. The cops weren't looking for him. He could talk his way out of...what? A ticket? A stolen vehicle charge?

Come to think of it, folks on the wrong side of the law would take matters in their own hands. She doubted they'd bring in the law.

Walking away without knowing what was about to happen to Rowan was the worst feeling. He was in this situation because of her. Not to mention the fact she was beginning to fall for the man. Rowan was the opposite of the kind of men she'd fallen for in the past. She'd mistaken a power grab for someone who wanted to protect and serve. She'd mistaken cockiness for confidence. Of course, the real traits of the men she'd been involved with up to now had been kept hidden in the early stages of her relationships. It made her not trust the feelings she had for Rowan. Time was the best predictor of how someone would act in the long run. Not rushing in or falling for someone who could be so charming in the beginning only to find out she'd fallen into the trap of a narcissist. Why was that quality so pervasive in the men she'd dated so far? They were so quick to pour on the charm. Now, it was a red flag.

Rowan was the opposite. He was real, honest, and made no apologies for being himself. Rowan was the real deal. Was he yet another person she cared about who would end up hurt on the sole basis of knowing her?

It took everything inside Tara not to double back to see what was going on in the SUV. The only thing stopping her was the fact Rowan had asked her to go. He was protecting her. Plus, honestly, she would only make the situation worse.

Why had the cop stopped them in the first place?

This whole scenario was suspicious. She searched her memory for any additional information about the SUV's owner Marcus Payne. The fact she'd heard the last name before, confirmed Xander knew this person. When he'd first approached her, her ex said he'd been between a rock and a hard place about using her dog spa for money laundering. He'd said there was no way out and it would be easier if she would go along with the Lieutenant's plan. She'd always assumed the Lieutenant meant someone on the job. What if Lieutenant was just a nickname rather than a rank?

If only she could get a look at the guy to know if she'd ever seen him before. The men who'd snatched her from Rowan's truck must work for him. Then again, if he was high ranking he wouldn't do the dirty work himself. *Payne.* Why was she drawing a blank on specifics?

Was it too late to go to the cops and plead her case? Once Grace was safely tucked away in a new rehab facility Tara could face the piper. She might end up going to jail for the rest of her life but nothing mattered as long as Grace was cared for.

Would it be too much to ask Rowan to check on Grace every once in a while?

There was a big problem with Tara's plan, she realized. Grace would be sick if she knew Tara was in prison. Would anyone believe Tara outside of Rowan and Grace? Certainly, the evidence would prove she was telling the truth, plus they had pictures to back up her story. Could she reach out to Officer Jenn McNeely? Would she be able to help? Offer advice?

The answer was most likely a resounding no.

What if the Lieutenant's men get to Xander first? Would they hide the evidence? Use it against her?

Greed did terrible things to people. Some people said money changed folks. Tara didn't buy it. Money allowed some folks to be who they were all along, in her opinion. It didn't create monsters out of good people. Take Rowan, for instance. He came from wealth but was the most down-to-earth person she'd probably ever met.

Tara entered the store, pushing her cart. Could she risk a glance back now? The rolling lights from the cop's SUV had ceased. Did that mean Rowan was free to go?

She turned to grab a sanitizing wipe. Out of the corner of her eye, she saw Rowan driving toward the door. Did he want her to come outside or stay put? The cop's SUV stayed parked where they'd been. What should she do?

This might be a mistake, but she returned the cart to the stock at the front of the store and headed out.

Rowan positioned the SUV so that the passenger door

faced the store. The move made it easy to climb into the seat while the bulk of the vehicle blocked her from the parking lot.

Tara claimed her seat and buckled in.

"New plan," Rowan said as he pulled away.

14

Rowan had barely finagled his way out of being taken down to the station for questioning. He'd been able to produce ID to prove he was not the owner of the vehicle and, therefore, the man with the warrant. "We're not parking behind the building. Not with this guy hanging around."

"What did he want?" Tara asked.

"Turns out, the driver of this vehicle has a warrant," he informed her. "It took some talking on my part but once I proved that I wasn't him, the cop let me go. By the way, the 'him' I'm referring to is Marcus Payne. The vehicle is registered to him. That much is confirmed."

Tara exhaled. "I keep trying to remember if there's anything else Xander said about Payne but keep drawing a blank."

"You're probably starving at this point," he said. "The brain likes to shut down when it needs food." He nodded toward the bags. "Go ahead and dig in. I'll eat as soon as I find a good spot to pull over."

"Only if you're sure you don't want me to wait," she offered.

"Food is getting cold," he said. "Go for it."

Tara pulled out a burger and then positioned a box of fries on the console. "This way, we can share."

He nodded and grabbed a couple of fries from the box.

The outskirts of town had fewer places to pitstop, so he pulled onto the lot of a diner near the highway and parked three-quarters of the way into the spaces where he'd be tucked between a rig and a Ford F-150 pickup.

Both devoured the burgers in record time. Rowan's coffee had gone cold but he didn't mind. It all tasted the same to him anyway. He wasn't particular as long as he got the caffeine fix.

"That's better," Tara said, leaning her head against the rest. "I had a nasty headache but this seems to have fixed it. Or calmed it down to a reasonable level at least."

"Lack of food doesn't do good things to the body or mind," he agreed.

Tara rolled her head to the left so she could look right at him. "What's our next move, Rowan?"

"First of all, we take a minute to think carefully about what we want to do," he said. Then, he remembered to make the request he'd meant to make earlier. "Hold on."

He picked up his cell and fired off a series of texts. Responses came back immediately.

His cell rang. Tanner.

"Hey," he said to his younger brother. The twins, Morgan and Nick, were two years older than Rowan who was smack dab in the middle with four brothers older and four younger. He was the ultimate middle child. The thought almost made him laugh.

"Where are you?" Tanner asked. The concern in his voice had Rowan sitting up a little straighter.

"In Colorado still. Why? Did something happen to our mother?" Rowan asked.

"I'm worried about you," Tanner said. "You take off without really telling anyone what you'll be doing or who you'll be with, and it's not like you."

"Like I said, I just needed to clear my head," Rowan said for the umpteenth time. The biggest problem with having a large family was having to repeat himself so much.

"I'm hearing rumors," Tanner admitted with trepidation in his voice.

"Plural?"

"Actually, one," Tanner said.

"Does it involve Alicia?" Rowan asked point blank. No sense skirting the issue.

"It does," Tanner said. "Is there any truth to it?"

"I guess there's always a chance," Rowan said. "About the same as a snowball's in hell, or at least close to it."

"Alright then," Tanner said with relief in his tone. "We still need you here."

"What's going on?" Rowan asked his brother, grateful for the change in subject. He didn't like his personal business spreading around on the rumor mill. It wasn't like Tanner be so persistent. "Did something happen?"

"Is that a serious question?" Tanner asked with a hint of frustration.

"Hey now," Rowan started. "We're all dealing with this the best we can. All I'm asking is if something else has gone down that I need to know about."

"No," Tanner said. "You know what? Never mind. I wanted to talk to my brother. Needed to talk to him about a whole lot of things but it seems like he's left the building and I'm chasing up the wrong tree to find him again."

What the hell?

"Tanner, you know I'd be there for you in a heartbeat if there was a reason to—"

"Forget I said anything."

The line went dead.

Rowan's finger hovered over the green button on his phone. Should he call Tanner back? Rather than do that while the situation was still hot, he called his brother Morgan instead. Morgan would be plugged into the details of what was happening with their brother.

"Rowan," Morgan said, picking up on the first ring. "Does this mean you're on your way home?"

Why was that everyone's first question? "Soon. Right now, I'm in the middle of something that I can't walk away from."

"Okayyy," Morgan said. "I saw the texts and we're on it. Do you have time to explain why you need these things?"

"Not right now," Rowan admitted. "I just got off the phone with Tanner, though. Anything I should know about that's going on with him? He sounded off."

"He reached out to you?" Morgan asked, clearly surprised.

"Just now," Rowan said. "And it didn't sound good."

"I'm caught off guard because he isn't talking to anyone right now," Morgan said.

Rowan was really shocked by his brother's comment. "That's strange because he gave me a hard time for being here and not at home."

"I'll go check on him," Morgan said on a sigh. "I'm not sure why he decided to pressure you but we all would like for you to be home. I'm not going to lie."

"To do what?" Rowan asked, hearing the frustration in his own tone. "Take a hospital shift? Pretend like we're all caring sons in a big, happy family?"

The line was quiet for a long moment.

"I'm outta line," Rowan conceded. "But this is exactly the reason I left. I'm not right with everything that's happened in the way I probably should be and I seriously doubt I'll be help to anyone right now." It was so much easier to immerse himself in someone else's problem.

"Take your time, man," Morgan said after a thoughtful pause. "There's no rush. I'm the one out of line for asking you to come back before you're ready."

"I appreciate it," Rowan said.

"You got it," Morgan said. "We'll see you when we see you. In the meantime, we're here for anything else you might need."

"Thanks," Rowan said. He still wasn't sold on the fact his brother understood but at least Morgan was making an effort.

"Take care of yourself," Morgan said. "We want your ugly self back home in one piece."

"You know it," Rowan said with a laugh, grateful for the break in tension. Teasing each other had been a favorite pastime of all the siblings and signaled they were in a good place. It was impossible to joke around with someone while tensions were high. Words and meanings were easily misconstrued and it was easy to take things the wrong way.

They ended the call after promising to stay in contact and saying goodbyes for the time being.

"Everything alright?" Tara asked almost immediately.

"I'm worried about one of my brothers," he said.

"Tanner," she said. "The one who called, right?"

He nodded.

"Any hint of what might be going on?" she asked.

"Afraid not," he supplied. "Guess it'll have to wait until I get back or at least until he cools off." Having been completely entrenched in Tara's situation, he hadn't given his own family much thought. Did that make him a jerk? "Everyone's dealing with more than anyone should have to back home."

"Because of what is going on with your mother?" she asked.

"That's right," he confirmed.

"Do you need to go back?" she asked. "Because as much as I appreciate you for it, helping me is putting you in danger." She paused a beat. "I couldn't live with myself if anything happened to you, Rowan."

∼

Tara meant what she'd said. Once her mom was out of harm's way, could she disappear for a while until it was safe to show her face again?

She'd killed a cop. There was no hiding from that reality. It was only a matter of time before a Be On The Lookout, BOLO, would be issued for her. If, in fact, there wasn't already one. The cop who'd pulled over Rowan didn't have a clue that she'd been with him. They'd tricked the police once. Would they be so lucky a second time?

Rowan leaned across the console until she turned to meet his gaze. He brought his hand up to her face and cupped her cheek, gently stroking her face with his thumb. "Hey. I'm here. I know what I'm doing. I've been in tricky situations before. Remember? I've tracked men as dangerous as these, believe it or not. Unfortunately, I'm better at tracking someone on our land than I am on city streets. We have a name. We can do some digging and possibly get an address. We'll have to ditch this vehicle here. It'll give away where we've been but one of the texts that I sent was to have my truck towed so we don't have to go back to the facility. Wheels are in motion and it's only a matter of time before we figure this thing out. Then, we'll both be able to take a step back and breathe again."

The circular motion of his thumb as he stroked her cheek was almost mesmerizing enough to make her forget how dire the situation truly was, and how easy it was going to be for her to end up dead or in jail.

"I killed a cop, Rowan," she heard the shakiness in her own voice. "It's only a matter of time before I'm arrested and locked behind bars. They'll throw away the key."

"I'm not going to allow that to happen," he said.

"Hope isn't something I can afford right now, Rowan."

With him this close, the air in the cab shifted from stress and fear to fire and chemistry. Love had been a foreign word to her before Rudy and Grace. The sense of belonging somewhere had been strange at first. Once she got used to it, she couldn't imagine family could be any different. The growing feelings she had for Rowan wasn't something she'd ever experienced before either. Would it set the bar so high no one else could ever reach it? Would it be the feeling she would seek out for the rest of her life and never quite achieve?

Would it matter while she rotted in a jail cell? Or worse, was murdered by inmates or prison guards. Hearing about Rowan's mother was a wake-up call. On second thought, dying might be a better alternative to the sentence she was going to face. But then there was Grace to think about. She wouldn't survive knowing Tara was locked up or gone forever. Who would look after her mom?

As for her feelings for Rowan...she would just have to learn to live without them.

Looking into his eyes, all she could think about right this second was how badly she wanted to kiss him.

"This might be a strange request under the circumstances," she began as she sucked in her bottom lip. It was her go-to move when she was nervous. She couldn't help but notice Rowan's gaze dropped to her lips. His parted ever so slightly. Just enough for her to get a peek at perfectly straight, white teeth.

"Go ahead," he finally said. "Ask me anything."

She quirked a brow. "Do you really mean that?"

"Yes," he said.

"Kiss me?"

He leaned a little closer to her lips. "I thought you'd never ask."

With that, he touched his lips to hers so gently the kiss robbed her breath. His thumb was still working its magic, causing an ache to form deep in her chest like she'd never experienced before. It was him. All him. And she wanted all of him.

Tara parted her lips before teasing his tongue inside her mouth. At first, he let the tip dart inside. The move caused more of that ache to rise up inside her, filling her, demanding from her.

She brought her hands up to cup his face as she bit down on his bottom lip.

Rowan groaned a deep, throaty growl that was the sexiest thing she'd ever heard. More ache welled up inside her, building, craving.

She hadn't needed someone in the way she needed Rowan in...ever. This moment might not last beyond tonight, so she had no plans to waste it. Time was precious and most definitely not on her side.

Before she knew it, Rowan was over the console. He reached around her and lowered the seat to almost lying down position. His heft on top of her made her wish for things she probably shouldn't from him.

He parted her thighs with his knees and positioned himself in the V of her legs. She felt his erection pressing against her. There were only two layers of denim between what she knew would be absolute rapture.

When he drove his tongue inside her mouth, she wrapped her legs around him.

The sound of voices broke them apart too soon. Before she could say, "Hold on," he was back in the driver's seat, straightening his shirt and pretending like they hadn't just experienced the most erotic moment of her life. There was so much more than physical attraction going on. Tara needed more than a pretty face. Although, Rowan certainly had that in spades. Beautiful might be a better word. The phrase *carved from granite* came to mind.

To reach this height of desire, there had to be so much more to a person. Intelligence was far sexier than a pretty face with an empty shell, like so many guys she'd known. Compassion was high on her list. Kindness was big. Honesty and humility didn't normally accompany such a perfect specimen of a man.

No. A man like Rowan Firebrand was almost impossible to find.

Was he perfect? Probably not. Although, she hadn't seen evidence to the contrary just yet. Then again, she barely knew him. Her heart wanted to argue otherwise, but she'd spent little more than twenty-four hours with him. Could she know someone on an intimate level so quickly? Logic argued no despite her heart's steadfast opinion.

Her brain wanted to make a case that she was simply a drowning woman grabbing hold of a life raft, and that was the only reason she felt a connection to Rowan. The two of them couldn't have come from more different backgrounds. She didn't even know his favorite color or his favorite foods.

It wasn't logical that she could have fallen in love with him. Was it?

15

Rowan was knee-deep in something he couldn't quite pinpoint. It felt a whole lot like love, except no love he'd ever known. The ideal of what love might be maybe. But this couldn't be the real thing. Could it? They didn't know each other. They had no history. And yet, it was as if they'd known each other on a soul level their entire lives.

Rather than sit here and wax poetic longer, he shifted his thoughts to something more productive. How the hell were they going to go up against a criminal ring and win? Tara was right. With her background, defending herself against killing a cop would be difficult at best and impossible at worst.

A couple walked past them to a vehicle parked a row back. He exhaled the breath he'd been holding. If that had been real trouble, would he have been prepared for it?

Not while he was lost...because that was the only word that seemed fit to describe a place he'd never experienced before with a woman.

He needed to keep his mind sharp and in the present if

he was going to keep Tara safe and find a way to stop her from going to jail. "At first light, we should head back up the mountain. See what we can find there."

"I was thinking the same thing," she said after clearing her throat.

He'd heard the raspy quality to his own voice a few seconds ago. Time to refocus. Because it would be a little too easy to fall down that slippery slope of love with Tara. He was intense. She was intense. Things would get intense between them. How would that work?

Rowan would go back to the ranch. He would take his rightful place again. He would step up and be the person his family needed him to be. What about Tara? Would she even want to come live at the ranch?

He was getting ahead of himself.

"Where do we sleep tonight?" Tara asked.

"That's a good question," he said. "Without supplies, we can't camp at the base of the mountain. Plus, it's too late."

"Where is your truck being towed?" she asked. She was onto something there.

"A-1 Tow is picking it up," he said. "Problem is the other guys know what my truck looks like."

Rowan's cell buzzed. He checked the screen. "Speak of the devil."

"What? What is it?"

He showed her the picture of his truck. The windshield was broken as was the driver's side window.

"The message says the truck was empty," he said, disgusted.

"They got all your supplies," she said.

"That's right."

"They'll recognize this SUV for certain," she pointed out.

"True," he said. "We're short on options, though." He checked the map feature on his phone, searching for alternatives to the lot he'd parked in yesterday at the base of the mountain. "I thought about grabbing a car service but I have no idea how much these folks know about me, especially now that they've no doubt dug around in my glovebox. With a good hacker and my name, they could track my purchases if I use a credit card. I have enough cash on me to get through a few days, but we can't rent a vehicle or use a car service."

"We could always do this the old-fashioned way," she said, hitching her thumb out.

"Hitchhike?"

"We could abandon this vehicle heading in the opposite direction," she said.

He liked where this was going. "Point it in the direction of Texas."

"My thoughts exactly," she agreed.

"Alright then," he said. "Let's grab a few hours of shuteye first."

Tara settled into the seat, lowering the back to a more comfortable position.

Rowan's brain worked overtime after he did the same. Plus, there was no such thing as being comfortable, when a steering wheel was jammed up against his knees. Normally, it wouldn't bother him but he was on alert tonight.

Not being able to brush his teeth wasn't exactly a great way to go to sleep. He had hamburger breath that had gone sour when mixed with coffee. In a couple of hours, he'd grab a few supplies from that big box store. They could grab showers at a highway rest stop. He was used to being out on the land for days on end in the heat but not being able to brush his teeth would bug him. Plus, he didn't want to stink up the cabin of the SUV. He'd learned to rough it without being barbaric.

He still had no idea how they were going to defend Tara against the charges that were certain to come. He was also beginning to understand the difficulty of overcoming a rough start in life. He'd been hard on his mother for her actions. She deserved to serve whatever time she got to repay her debt to society. A line had been crossed with her being beaten in jail.

Getting her trial successfully relocated to Houston had been his future sister-in-law's biggest accomplishment to date. Avril was set to marry Morgan, so she was having herself removed from the case. Conflict of interest dictated she take a step back once she got engaged to her client's son. However, she was able to secure the best seasoned defense attorney in Texas. David Lawrence had taken more high-profile cases than any other, and had won. Rowan didn't believe his mother should get off scot-free. She'd done the crime and needed to do the time. But she also deserved to be protected from bullies while doing so. Once he returned to his home state, he planned to visit her to see if she'd learned her lesson like the others believed she had. Or if she was lost forever.

Cutting his own mother off wasn't something Rowan ever believed he would do, despite his upbringing. If she showed no remorse, though, what choice would he have?

Right now, he needed to focus on how he was going to get Tara out of her current situation. Grace would be moved to a secure nursing home in Texas in two hours. The place was as close to the ranch as he could get, in case Tara ended up serving time. The least he could do for her was take care of Grace. If she was close to the ranch, he could do that a whole lot easier. Bronc Harris was ranch foreman. He'd been with the family for as long as Rowan could remember. Bronc arranged the pickup and relocation of Grace for Rowan, according to Morgan. Her identity would be protected while she was airlifted to Rehab Acres outside of Austin.

Once Rowan received a text confirming the relocation was complete, he would share the news with Tara. At this point, his stress levels were through the roof, knowing the transfer was about to take place. A lot could go wrong on an operation like this.

By the time Tara woke up, he hoped to be able to provide good news. It would mean a lot to her and he wanted to be able to deliver something that would put a smile on her face even if it was only temporary. And it would be short-lived with the day they had planned.

An hour passed as Rowan stayed lost in thought. He could go without sleep for days when needed. Plus, his mind kept churning. Could he do a little digging into the background of Marcus Payne?

He dimmed the light on his cell so as not to wake Tara and then searched for the name Marcus Payne.

There were no results that applied after scrolling. Desperation was starting to kick in. They couldn't be on the run for long without being stopped again. This vehicle was hot. Risking one of his family member's life to ask someone to pick them up was not even a serious consideration. Rowan had better not use his credit card in case the criminal ring had picked up his name when they'd ransacked his truck.

Maybe he should have expected it, but it still frustrated him to no end. There'd been a crowd standing around the lot so the perps would have had to have come back. Or probably called for reinforcements. Then, there was the matter of the perp's cell phone. Turning it into the law could corroborate Tara's story, in theory at least. It was an important piece of evidence they needed to hang onto.

Hours passed as he sat there, wishing for a break. He was overthinking the situation, which meant answers would run in the opposite direction. Since he needed to stop off at the box store the minute doors opened, he put his seat up and then started the engine.

Traffic was almost nothing as he navigated onto the roadway.

At least Tara still slept. She'd been through more than any one person should have to in one lifetime. She needed —no, *deserved*—a break.

He parked on the side of the building next to what he figured were employee vehicles.

Tara's seat was down. She wasn't visible from the outside, unless someone walked right up to the SUV.

Leaving Tara alone was a risk he needed to take. Rowan walked inside the building and then located enough supplies to get through a couple of days, including a much-needed change of clothing for both of them. He'd had to guess at her size. After checking out in the self-check aisle, he practically gaited toward the SUV.

Rowan's heart plummeted to his boots when he got there. Tara was gone.

~

TARA WASHED her face in the bathroom of the big box store. She needed a toothbrush and toothpaste but all she could do was rinse her mouth at this point. After using the facilities, she made her way back to the SUV, keeping her chin down and making eye contact with no one.

Rounding the corner of the building, she saw an extremely stressed-out Rowan pacing around the SUV.

With a dire look on his face, he turned to her and made a beeline toward her. "I didn't know if something happened to you."

"I'm here," she reassured. The look caused guilt to slam into her. She hadn't meant to worry him, especially after all they'd been through together. "I had to use the restroom. That's all. I figured I could make it back before you finished your purchases."

Rowan pulled her into an embrace. He peppered kisses on her forehead, her cheek, and then grazed her lips. "I thought I lost you."

Tara hated putting him through hell. She honestly believed she would beat him back to the SUV or she would have figured out a way to leave a note or something. "I should have tried to wait. I didn't know how long you'd be and I had to use the restroom like nobody's business."

Rowan exhaled. "When this is behind us, we need to have a discussion."

"About?" she asked but he had already linked their fingers and was walking toward the second row door of the SUV.

He stopped and opened it without answering her question, letting go of her hand in the process. "I bought enough to last a few days. Figured you'd want to brush your teeth as much as I do."

"Sounds like heaven about now," she admitted. "Should I take the bag in the bathroom with me?"

"Figured we could brush here and spit next to the tree," he said. "I'd rather not let you out of my sight again, if that's alright with you."

She could admit the few minutes they'd been apart had weighed heavily on her too. "I'd like that."

Rowan handed over supplies along with a bottle of water.

Clean teeth and a fresh month were not to be taken for granted. They worked miracles. There was something about those little things, simple acts that were good for the soul during stressful times.

"We can stop off for coffee," Rowan said. "I picked up a few power bars if you're starving."

"I can wait," she said as they reclaimed their seats. "Plus, it might be nice to save them as long as possible." She did, however, polish off a bottle of water in a matter of a minute. She would no longer take anything for granted once this ordeal was behind her.

Who was she kidding? This would follow her the rest of her life. Xander was dead by her hands. Another involuntary shiver rocked her body. He might not have turned out to be the person she'd believed him to be, but that didn't take away from the fact he should be alive right now.

Why did he have to come after her? Follow her? Why couldn't he have accepted a breakup and let both of them move on with their lives?

Men like him were sore losers, a little voice in the back of her mind reminded her. Not only had she flat-out refused to let him launder money for a criminal organization through her business, but she'd personally rejected him by saying she wanted out of the relationship. His ego couldn't take it, so he'd come at her. He'd told her that he could force her to bend to his will. He'd planned to hurt Grace if Tara didn't listen and do exactly as he said.

Tara released a long, slow breath, trying to work some of the tension out of her body. She was safe for the time being here with Rowan. He had no plans to let anyone get to her. It was a promise they both knew he might not be able keep, but she appreciated it nonetheless.

After stopping for fast food breakfast and downing coffee, they hit a rest stop for showers and a change of clothes.

"I feel half human again," Tara said to him. Being with Rowan made her feel something else too. Something she wasn't ready to lean into or define.

"It's the little things," he said as a text came through on his phone. He glanced at it while stopped at a red light. "It's good news." He smiled before continuing. "Grace has been safely moved to a rehab facility in Texas."

"What? How?" she asked, literally in shock. "When did this happen?"

"I didn't want to say anything until the transfer was complete," he said.

"That's amazing," she said, trying to absorb the news her mom was safe. This was the first bit of good news since this whole ordeal started. A couple of happy tears spilled out of her eyes. "I'm not sure how you pulled it off or how I'll ever repay you, but thank you from the bottom of my heart."

"That's all I need to hear," he said before reaching over to squeeze her hand.

"We'll figure out something," she said as a couple more of those tears rolled down her cheeks. "This is more than anyone could have ever asked for."

"You never would ask," he pointed out.

"Doesn't mean I'm not grateful now," she said, meaning those words with her whole heart.

Grace was safe. Tara repeated those words a few times in her head to try to get them to stick. Her number one concern was now taken care of. It also meant she could disappear for a while until the heat was off. Or could she?

A cop had been killed in cold blood and left on a mountain. She could run all she wanted or face the music. Running would only buy time. Time to do what? As a fugitive, she wouldn't be able to work. She could kiss her dog spa business goodbye.

Or she could stay and fight.

"I want you to know that I'll look after Grace no matter what else happens," Rowan said as they neared the national forest.

"You have no idea how much I appreciate it," she said as more tears welled in her eyes.

"I think I have a good idea," he said. "Let's see what we're dealing with up the mountain and then we'll come up with a definitive plan for how to move forward. One of my future sisters-in-law is a defense attorney. Once we get the lay of the land, we can call her for advice."

Tara's chest squeezed thinking about walking up to a dead body. Would animals have already picked at Xander's lifeless body?

"Okay," she said absently, unable to concentrate on anything else but what they were about to encounter.

Rowan parked off-road instead of in a lot. The area was a viewing spot that sat about a quarter of the way up the mountain.

They made the trek to where she fled the scene in an hour and a half's time. It was cold this morning despite full sun.

Coming around from a different direction made keeping her bearings tricky, especially with all the new snow that had been dumped the night before last. Being anywhere near Xander's dead body was a sobering thought. One that would haunt her forever.

It was easy to see why Rowan was a successful tracker as they climbed over fallen tree trunks and down ravines. He stayed the course and kept them on the right path until they came over the top of the spot.

Snow covered any possible blood on the ground. Splatter on the trees was a dead giveaway this was the right area. Xander's body was gone.

16

"What does this mean?" Tara's voice shook as she asked the question.

"Could mean a number of things," Rowan began, his wheels were already turning. "For one, he might not have been dead."

"I checked his breathing," she said. "I know for a fact he'd stopped."

"You might have been mistaken or he could have been holding his breath," Rowan pointed out. "It's possible he hoped you'd panic and take off running. His experience would certainly help predict your behavior if you believed he was dead."

She opened her mouth to speak and then clamped it shut again, studying the area even more carefully as she walked circles around the spot.

Rowan checked his cell phone. "I have a couple of bars here. He might have called for help."

"Or been tracked here when he didn't report back to the Lieutenant," she pointed out.

"That's another option," he agreed. "They might not

want his body to be found just yet, or he could be alive and recovering. No matter what else happened, he took hard blows. There's a lot of blood here on the trees."

"Which is another reason I think for certain he was dead," she said as she rubbed her temples. "Everything happened so fast though."

"It's possible his breathing was shallow and that he was the one who ended up calling for help," Rowan pointed out. "There aren't any tracks leading here in the snow so he would have left the area or been picked up before the snowstorm intensified."

Tara caught his gaze and held it. "You know what this means?"

"You're not a cop killer," he said.

Tara paced around the site. "This might just be the best thing that could have happened, now that I really think about it."

"You might be free of any possible charges against you," he said.

"Maybe I should try to call Xander," she said. "I didn't think about it before because...well, you know exactly why I didn't. But now." Wide-eyed, she took a deep breath. "Now, he might be alive."

True. There were good reasons not to make that call while out here. If Rowan's identity still happened to be secret, he didn't want his name to get out. "I'd rather not use my phone to make the call."

"Of course not," came the immediate response. "And I don't want him anywhere near you."

Rowan had something to say about that. "Easier said than done because I'm not leaving your side until you get your life back. That's a promise."

Tara walked over to him and pressed a kiss to his lips.

"Isn't that precious?" an unfamiliar male voice boomed from behind them.

"Xander?" Tara said as her face turned bleached-sheet white. She spun around, searching for the source. "Where are you?"

Rowan turned toward the voice before tucking Tara behind him. Even with the echo, he tracked it east.

"Is this who you left me for?" Xander asked with disgust.

"You're alive," Tara said with a note of disbelief in her tone.

"You tried to kill me, bitch," Xander spit out. "But you weren't strong enough. You're weak and no amount of self-defense classes would make you a match for me. Now, it's your turn to die."

"Hold on," Rowan whispered, backing them up until a tree trunk could shield them.

The crack of a bullet split the air. Shrapnel took a chunk out of the tree next to their heads. Rowan bit back a curse.

"We need to head down," he continued. "Zigzag through the trees so it'll be harder for him to hit his mark."

"Okay," Tara said before turning and wasting no time moving.

A few steps into their descent, the pair of guys from the SUV last night moved into their line of sight. Essentially, Xander and the two guys had formed a triangle around them. This made escaping next to impossible without running into one of the men.

"Trap them," Xander commanded, clearly the one in charge. Rowan still couldn't get a good look at the man but he'd like to be within arm's reach so he could throw a punch.

The triangle started shrinking, making escape without

coming into close contact with at least one of the men next to impossible. Rowan released a string of curses.

Trees would provide some cover. Would they be enough? Since the situation wasn't looking good, Rowan palmed his cell and then tapped 911. He turned the volume way down.

"Hey, Lieutenant," Voice One shouted. "What do you want us to do with these bitches?"

"Lieutenant?" Tara asked, stepping out from behind Rowan. He tried to shield her but she wanted to be seen. "Xander? *You're* the Lieutenant?"

"I told you not to speak, Marcus," Xander shouted. Marcus Payne. The driver of the SUV. Now, they had two perps identified. Now, they only needed to know who the third was to make certain all three were brought to justice.

"Yeah?" Marcus said. "You said she'd break as soon as you put a little pressure on her and her mother but look where we are now."

"Shut the hell up," Xander demanded.

While the call was in progress and Xander was busy arguing with Marcus, Rowan flipped his cell to camera mode and turned on video mode. He hit the red button, darkened the screen and tucked the phone inside his jacket pocket. He already knew it was possible to get bars here, so he hoped the call had gone through and someone was listening.

"I can't believe you deceived me like that, Xander. It was you all along." Anger caused Tara's voice to shake. "You were the one who wanted to launder money through my store. You sonofabitch. You wanted to ruin my business and my life. Possibly send me to jail. And then what? You'd be the cop hero? Would you have been the one to arrest me too?"

Rowan tugged at her hand. "Let's go." He had no idea if

and when help would arrive. At the very least, Xander would be seen for the criminal he was.

"Hold on," she said to Rowan, keeping her attention on Xander. "You were willing to betray me all the while pretending to love me? Not that what we shared was love in any shape or form. But still."

"Like you should talk," Xander shot back. "How much could you have ever loved me if you jumped in this man's bed so fast?"

As far as Rowan was concerned, those were fighting words.

"Hold on there," Rowan cut in. "What we do or don't do is none of your business."

"You're forgetting the fact anything that has to do with *my woman* is my business," Xander quipped.

Rowan grabbed Tara's shoulders to stop her from storming the bastard. The words, *my woman,* were the equivalent of fingernails on a chalkboard.

"I'm not your property and never was," Tara bit out. "If you know what's best, you'll turn yourself in because I sure as hell plan to make sure your supervising officer knows what you've been up to. Money laundering at my shop was probably just the tip of the iceberg of your illegal dealings."

"What do you know about what I do?" Xander demanded. "I lived under the same roof and you didn't figure it out. No one else will either. Not unless I tell them myself. And no one will take your word over mine."

"That's where you're wrong," Rowan said, pulling his cell out of his pocket and holding it in the air. "Do you see this? I've been on the phone with law enforcement this whole time. They've heard everything, Xander Smythe. There's no turning back now."

Xander shouted more than a few curses.

"We're not part of this," Marcus said. "Come on, Reggie. Let's go."

The sounds of footsteps followed. Rowan tensed as he waited to hear a shot fired. When none came, he grabbed Tara and positioned them both behind a tree.

"We can put a stop to this right now," he whispered to her. "Stay close to me, though. I don't want him getting anywhere near you. And I sure don't want him using you as a hostage to escape the law."

"Were you serious about the call?" she asked, her gaze dropped to the cell in his hand.

"Yes," he confirmed. "No idea if the call made it through or was dropped at some point."

She grabbed hold of his hand and put the cell up to her mouth. "My name is Tara Dowling and I'm the former girlfriend of Alexander Smythe. He goes by Xander. He tried to coerce me into laundering money through my small business. When I refused, he came after me. I've been in hiding until he chased me into this forest where I managed to knock him out in self-defense. He goes by the name Lieutenant and he's here now trying to kill me and Rowan Firebrand and—"

A shot echoed from above. A bullet fragment slammed into the tree two feet away from them.

"If you can hear me, please help us," she added before letting go of his hand.

"He'll follow us if we try to get away," Rowan said after losing a visual. "I'm going to him."

"He'll kill us both," Tara warned. "He has no conscience."

"Wait here," he said. "I don't want you coming with me."

Rowan didn't wait for a reaction. He pressed his cell into

the palm of her hand and then took off in the direction of the shot.

~

TARA NEEDED TO CREATE A DIVERSION, so she started running down the hill. "You never truly had me, Xander. And you never will. And there's nothing you can do about it." Those words would challenge him. Anger him. She was betting on the fact his ego would take over and he would give chase. Xander was a hothead.

Rowan, on the other hand, was the definition of stealth and calm. She'd lost visual on him almost immediately. Not to mention hadn't heard so much as a peep.

Another shot rang out, causing her to trip and fall. She grabbed a low branch on the way down. At least some of her fall was broken by the branch. The phone went flying. She searched, feeling around for it in the needles. Tara covered a gasp. Please tell her she didn't lose Rowan's cell and their only link to the outside world. He'd made the call to 911 but there hadn't been confirmation that someone had picked up or that the call wasn't dropped due to the patchy reception.

Had she just lost their chance at ensuring justice was served? Would they both die in vain?

The sounds of footsteps coming her way pushed her to her feet. She needed to keep going.

"Where are you, bitch?" Xander screeched, more than a hint of desperation in his voice now that his buddies had abandoned him.

"I'm right here," she fired back. It was probably not her brightest move but it was too late to reel it in now. Besides, she wanted to keep Xander's attention on her instead of Rowan's whereabouts.

Time had run out to search for the cell, so she abandoned the effort.

Running in a zigzag pattern, she pushed her legs as fast as they could go until her thighs burned and her lungs clawed for air.

Xander had run past the spot where her and Rowan last stood behind the tree. She couldn't exactly shout out to him. A dark thought hit. Had he been shot? Was he lying on the mountain somewhere bleeding out?

Tara squeezed her eyes shut and tried to will her pulse to return to a reasonable pace. As it was, however, running wild. Pain ripped through her thighs as she descended the mountain. Another thought hit. Would she catch up to the other bastards before they made it down? For all she knew, she could be running right into them. Their exit might have been a trick to lure Tara and Rowan down the mountain.

It was quiet above her except for the sounds of Xander's occasional laugh.

"I'm coming for you. No one can save you now," he threatened. "No one cares about you. I was all you had and now you're alone. And *mine* despite what you might think."

His ligament tear was the only thing keeping him from catching her. She was certain of the fact. If Xander was in full form, this chase would have been over almost before it started.

But where was Rowan?

17

Rowan descended the mountain parallel with Xander with a safe distance. If Marcus and Reggie had actually left and that wasn't a trap, Rowan liked his odds of going one on one with Xander.

Crouching low, he stalked Xander's movements like a predator stalks prey. The bastard was fixated on Tara, but a cop was not to be underestimated. Plus, Rowan had no idea if his call to 911 had gone through so they might be out here on their own with no backup on the way. He could hope for the best but he had to plan for the worst.

Rowan circled around. He was faster than Xander and, from the looks of it, had more experience in the outdoors. He'd lean into any advantage he could. It's what made him a good tracker.

The day was kicking into high gear. Clouds had rolled in and along with them a chilly breeze. The twigs and sticks covering the ground made it difficult to move without making a sound.

Tara had done a good job of provoking Xander. And now

Rowan would continue to use the distraction to his advantage.

A clearing was up ahead. It was the point where Xander would most likely catch up to her. He'd holstered his weapon in order to run faster as he favored his right knee. The holster move was working even though Tara had a head start.

She was quick too. And he remembered how good she was at turning a situation around to her advantage. The two unknowns were out there somewhere, Marcus and Reggie. They'd scattered like buckshot, which didn't mean they wouldn't have a change of heart and turn around. The Lieutenant was powerful and, now that they knew he was Xander, a cop. Sticky didn't begin to describe this situation.

"What's wrong, Xander? Can't you run very fast after losing all that blood?" Tara taunted. "You always were a little weak."

"You're a bitch," he said. "I should have known better than to get twisted up with you. Once worthless trash, always worthless trash."

She laughed. The sound echoed. And it seemed to only ignite the fire.

Xander wouldn't forget about Rowan. There was no chance of it but he was distracted, so Rowan needed to capitalize on the moment.

He waited for the right moment. *Patience.*

Xander had Tara in his sights. Another ten seconds and he would be right on top of her. Rowan couldn't allow that to happen.

He sprang from his position, launching himself onto Xander's back. The stunned perp took a couple of steps forward as he reached for his weapon. Let him get to his Glock and this fight would be over before it started.

Could Rowan beat him to it?

Rowan tried and failed but he managed to grab Xander's hand and force it above his head as they landed and then skidded a couple of feet down the mountain. Rowan lost visual contact with Tara while he struggled to maintain control of the situation.

Xander rolled like an alligator with prey in its jaws, knocking Rowan off. Momentum caused him to roll out of reach. Rowan scrambled to his hands and knees before Xander could get hold of the butt of his gun.

Rowan reared back and punched Xander, whose hand instinctively shot up to block. Rowan's fist connected with the side of Xander's head. All Rowan could think about at this point was being around for Tara. If anything happened to him, she would be left stranded and alone. That couldn't be allowed to happen.

He used the rage building inside him to throw another punch.

Xander fought back, as expected. He had grabby hands, which he used to squeeze Rowan's neck. The guy was a fighter.

Rowan managed to get a foot in between him and Xander. Using a tree behind as anchor, Rowan pushed against Xander's chest until his grip broke. Rowan coughed, trying to get air in his lungs again.

Tara was there in his peripheral. She had a boulder in her hands that she held high above her head. Given the right moment, she would slam it into Xander.

But the cop was quick. He saw what was going on and swept her feet with his arm, knocking her off balance. The big rock came flying toward Rowan, who deflected it with his forearm. It hurt like hell, but the boulder missed his head, which was far more important than a bruise on his arm.

Xander went for Tara.

She let out a scream as she locked his head in her arm. With her free hand, she threw several wild punches.

Xander laughed as he caught her fist.

The distraction gave Rowan a chance to regroup. He popped to his feet, grabbed the boulder, and then slammed the rock into the back of Xander's head. Xander's body went limp as Rowan unholstered the man's weapon and checked around for Marcus and Reggie. It was almost too good to hope they'd truly abandoned the mountain situation.

"Call for help," he said to Tara.

"I lost your phone on the way down," she said in between gasps for air.

"I'll sit on the bastard while you go find it," he said, rolling Xander face down. Rowan mounted the guy's back and squeezed powerful thighs to keep his arms by his sides in case he came to again ready to fight.

Underestimating Xander would be a mistake Rowan had no plans to make.

The squawk of a police radio echoed. Rowan tensed. He had no idea if the law would be friendly or see him as a threat to a fellow officer.

On balance, he had to take the risk. "Up here."

Tara caught on and began jumping up and down while waving her hands in the air. "Help us. Please. Somebody. We've been attacked."

"Do you see anyone?" he asked.

"Not yet," she said. "Hold on. Wait. There. I see someone making their way up the mountain. There's two of them." She waved her arms again. "Up here. Please."

A couple of minutes later, the first officer arrived on the

scene. He was tall and skinny with a runner's build. "Hands where I can see 'em."

"Yes, sir," Rowan said, holding the Glock high in the air where the officer could keep a visual.

Tara's hands went up and stayed up. "We are the ones who called 911. This officer is Alexander Smythe."

"Yes, ma'am," the first officer confirmed as a second one, female, arrived. Next, a forest ranger joined in.

"Jenn?" Tara said as tears rolled down her cheeks. "Or should I say, Officer McNeely?"

"Call me Jenn," the female officer said as she walked straight over to Tara. "It's over. You did it." Jenn pulled Tara into a hug. "I came as soon as I heard it was you. I knew something was up for a long time with Xander. He doesn't deserve to wear the badge."

The ranger walked over to Rowan and relieved him of the Glock. "We heard everything on the radio. You're all safe now."

Rowan slowly stood up, keeping his hands high in the air. "What about the others? There were two men."

"They were apprehended at the base of the mountain, sir," the first officer said. "They're already promising to testify against this officer for a lighter sentence."

"It's over?" Tara asked.

"Yes, ma'am," the officer said.

Xander shook his head and blinked his eyes open. His gaze shot to his fellow officer. "Fielding, these two assaulted me. Why aren't they in cuffs?"

"We know what you've done, Xander," Officer Fielding said. "You're going to jail."

Xander's wild gaze shifted to the female officer. "Jenn? You know they're lying about me. Whatever they're saying, it isn't true and can't be proved."

A satisfied smile broke across Jenn's face. "You've been suspect for a long time, Xander. You're going down."

Rowan exhaled a slow breath before giving his statement. Tara was taken to the side by the ranger to give her account.

"Do either of you need medical assistance?" Officer Fielding asked when statements had been given.

"No, sir," Rowan confirmed.

"We'll be taking this one to jail," Officer Fielding said, forcing Xander to his feet. His zip-cuffed hands locked behind him. He sneered at Tara as he walked past.

"Keep smiling," Tara said sarcastically. "I know I am."

"He won't get away with this," Jenn reassured.

The officers and ranger began their descent down the mountain as Tara sat down next to Rowan and leaned her head on his shoulder.

The conversation they needed to have couldn't wait any longer but he had no idea how she was about to react to what he had to say.

∽

"It's over," Tara said as Rowan wrapped an arm around her shoulder. She could scarcely believe the nightmare was over.

"We need to talk," Rowan said. His unsure tone caught her attention. Was he about to walk out of her life?

"I know," she said, pre-empting him. The last thing she needed was to hang onto something that never had a chance anyway.

"You do?"

"Yes," she confirmed. "Of course, we do." She sat a little straighter. "You've done so much for me and my mom. I want to find a way to repay the debt and don't give me that pay it forward line, because that only works when you owe for a cup of coffee or lunch. What you've done is huge and it deserves to be recognized as such."

"I can think of one thing that will wipe away the debt of gratitude," he said. His steady, even voice gave away nothing of where this might be going.

"That's great," she said. "It'll be clear cut that way. Besides, I don't like to go through life owing people."

"Good," he agreed. "We're on the same page then."

"Yes," she said, a little caught off guard by his quick agreement. "We are."

"Then, I have a proposal," he began as he turned to catch her gaze. Looking into those beautiful eyes of his would melt anyone's heart, so she wasn't surprised when it melted hers.

"Let's hear it," she said.

"That was it," he said with dry crack of a smile.

She cocked an eyebrow unsure of where this was headed. "What's the proposal?"

He didn't respond.

"It's customary to finish your sentence," she urged.

"I did," he said looking smug and a little bit nervous at the same time, an interesting combination. He took her hand in his. "I can't exactly bend down on one knee, but I'd be honored if you would agree to marry me."

Her mouth literally dropped to the ground.

"I know what you're thinking," he continued, looking a little thrown off at her reaction. "We don't know each other well enough to make a commitment like that. So, I'm willing to wait however long it takes until you feel like you know me. If it takes the rest of our lives for you to say yes, I'm good with that, as long as I get to be with you in the meantime."

"Are you serious?" she asked after she picked her mouth up off the ground.

"I've never been more serious about anything in my life, Tara. I never thought my life was missing a thing until I met you. The pieces, you and me, just fit, and I don't need a year of dating or whatever timeframe folks think is acceptable to know that I want to spend the rest of my life with you. You're smart and beautiful. You're kind and have a heart bigger than my home state. And you've got a spirit on you that belongs running wild with the horses. I would never try to tame it, because I'm in love with you just the way you are. You're perfect and I couldn't be more in love with anyone than I am with you."

Tears welled in Tara's eyes as she listened to the words that she felt in her heart.

"I feel the same way about you, Rowan," she stated. "I'll never meet a better person or more perfect match. I've fallen in love with you too. And I'd be honored to become your wife."

"Permission to kiss my future bride," Rowan said with that same smile that was so good at seducing her.

She beat him to the punch. She kissed the love of her life. She couldn't have found a better person to love and do life with than Rowan Firebrand.

There was no reason to wait. In her book, their life together began right now. And she couldn't be happier for it.

18

EPILOGUE

Tanner Firebrand paced the hallway at the hospital, waiting for his brother's return to Lone Star Pass. He had information that would change Rowan's life, but this news wasn't something to be delivered over the phone. Besides, Rowan was on his way to the hospital, which he'd said was a necessary pitstop since he had yet to visit their mother.

Sitting on life-changing news was the most difficult thing Tanner had had to do in a long time. Then again, difficult was a pretty good word to describe life in general at the ranch. He'd like to say this was new but he'd be lying. They'd had a difficult upbringing. They'd had difficult parents. And now they were in a difficult position with their mother ever since she broke down and attempted murder to gain more of the family money from Tanner's grandfather.

Was it any surprise him and his brothers were sick to death of money?

Rowan had news of his own, or so he'd said.

"Hey," his brother's voice yanked Tanner from his revelry.

Rowan brought Tanner into a hug. "I mentioned a surprise."

Tanner's gaze shifted to the woman who'd stopped a couple of feet away. "Not you too."

"I guess so." Rowan laughed. He walked over to the woman and took her hand. "This is Tara Dowling, my fiancée."

"Figures," Tanner said under his breath as he took the couple of steps to close the distance between them. He extended a hand, which she vigorously shook. "Congratulations, and welcome to the family."

"You don't have to sound like you just welcomed her to a funeral," Rowan stated with a chuckle.

"Apologies, ma'am," Tanner said. He genuinely felt guilty if he'd come across that way. "I don't have anything against fiancées or marriage as long as they involve someone else."

Tara laughed. She was beautiful, he'd give her that much. Why she would want to marry into his messed up family was anybody's guess. "What's wrong? Not the marrying kind?"

"No, ma'am," he said with a tip of his hat. "No disrespect intended."

"It would take a whole lot more than that to offend me," she quipped. There was a sparkle to her eyes that told him she could fend for herself in an argument. Good. She needed to be strong to get by in this family.

"Why do I have a feeling you're going to do just fine around here?" Tanner asked with a half grin.

"I'll take that as a compliment," Tara said as her violet eyes lit up.

"Good," he said. That was how he meant it to come across. Tanner turned his attention to his brother. He had no idea if Tara was familiar with Rowan's 'situation' but he didn't want to be the one to tip her off. "Mind if I have a word with you alone?"

"Anything you have to say to me can be said in front of my—"

"I need a cup of coffee," Tara interrupted. Her stock just went up a couple of notches with Tanner. She seemed to know when it was a good time to bow out of a conversation and he appreciated her for it. "Anyone else care for one?"

"None for me," Tanner said. "If I have anymore, the floor will start shaking."

"That'd be nice," Rowan said before kissing his bride-to-be.

Tanner turned around real quick and looked in the opposite direction. He gave the lovebirds a moment of privacy. Marriage was spreading like a virus within the family. He wanted nothing to do with it. The running joke was that there was something in the water. He'd taken to drinking the imported kind in a bottle to avoid any chance of becoming infected.

"What did you want to talk to me about?" Rowan asked, coming up beside Tanner.

He glanced behind him to make sure Tara wasn't within listening distance. When he was certain she was out of earshot, he said, "Alicia lied about being pregnant. There's no baby."

"How do you know there ever was one?" Rowan asked, clearly caught off guard.

"This is a small town and—"

"Are you fixing to tell me other people are in on this too?" Rowan asked as he stabbed his fingers in his hair.

"No," Tanner said. "As far as I know, it's just me and BethAnne."

"BethAnne from middle school?" Rowan asked.

"Well, yes, but more importantly, BethAnne from the obstetrician's office," Tanner informed. "She's a nurse and used to be friends with Alicia until she pulled this stunt. BethAnne said she wanted to come to you herself, but Alicia made her promise not to say anything until she could come clean about the lie."

Rowan exhaled long and slow. "There's no possibility that I'm a father?"

Tanner shook his head but then locked gazes with his brother. "Are you disappointed? Because I didn't see that coming."

"No," Rowan quickly reassured. "I couldn't be happier." He paused a couple of beats like he had to figure out his thoughts so he could explain himself. "I never wanted to be a father before now. Before Tara. It's weird too because I would have never guessed in a million years that I might change my mind about something this big."

"Does Tara want kids?" Tanner asked.

"Not that I'm aware of," Rowan said. "Which makes my reaction even stranger." He issued a sharp sigh. "Here's the thing. I don't want to have kids with Alicia. She was a liar and a cheat, and I wish I'd seen it coming before but honestly I've been too involved in our own family drama since our grandfather died to see her for who she was." He planted his hands on his hips. "But with Tara, I could see raising a family."

All Tanner could do was shake his head.

"What?"

"I've seen this look a little too often recently," he said. "That doe-eyed, I've-met-the-love-of-my-life look. It's fine. It suits you, which surprises me even more." He backed away a couple of steps. "But I want nothing to do with it. You hear?"

"That's your choice, man," Rowan said with a chuckle.

"What are you laughing at?" Tanner asked.

"I said almost those exact same words before meeting Tara," Rowan informed. He could keep that information to himself.

"This affects me in what way?" Tanner quipped.

"None," Rowan said with another one of those annoying chuckles.

"I'm happy for you and Tara," Tanner said. "Believe it. I see something in you that I've never seen before. It's good. Don't get me wrong. But that's you and the others. That's not me. Plus, there's still a few of us left who still have our heads on straight."

More of that laughter came and then Rowan's mood shifted to something far more serious. He nodded toward their mother's room. "How is she?"

"Doing better," Tanner said. "She was beat up pretty badly but nothing permanent."

"After hearing her story and what she went through as a kid, it's damn hard to stay mad at her," Rowan admitted.

"Then don't," Tanner said.

Rowan's eyebrow arched. "Are you telling me that you've forgiven her?"

"I'm not here to be her judge and jury," Tanner said. "She messed up big time. What she attempted to do was wrong on so many levels that I can't even begin to reconcile it. But who am I to turn my back on her?"

"She's been through hell and back," Rowan agreed. "That's for sure."

"I highly doubt any of us would ever go down the same path as her, but I'm certainly not perfect," Tanner stated. "All I know is that we have to stick together because she might end up in jail for the rest of her life. How are we going to handle that?"

"One day at a time, I guess," Rowan surmised. "It's the best anyone can do."

Tanner nodded. His brother was right. "You ready to go inside?"

Another deep breath came before his brother said, "It's time."

To keep reading Tanner's story, click here.

ALSO BY BARB HAN

Texas Firebrand

Rancher to the Rescue

Disarming the Rancher

Rancher under Fire

Rancher on the Line

Undercover with the Rancher

Rancher in Danger

Set-Up with the Rancher

Rancher Under the Gun

Taking Cover with the Rancher

Firebrand Cowboys

VAUGHN: Firebrand Cowboys

RAFE: Firebrand Cowboys

MORGAN: Firebrand Cowboys

NICK: Firebrand Cowboys

ROWAN: Firebrand Cowboys

TANNER: Firebrand Cowboys

Don't Mess With Texas Cowboys

Texas Cowboy's Protection

Texas Cowboy Justice

Texas Cowboy's Honor

Texas Cowboy Daddy

Texas Cowboy's Baby

Texas Cowboy's Bride

Texas Cowboy's Family

Texas Cowboy Sheriff

Texas Cowboy Marshal

Texas Cowboy Lawman

Texas Cowboy Officer

Texas Cowboy K9 Patrol

Cowboys of Cattle Cove

Cowboy Reckoning

Cowboy Cover-up

Cowboy Retribution

Cowboy Judgment

Cowboy Conspiracy

Cowboy Rescue

Cowboy Target

Cowboy Redemption

Cowboy Intrigue

Cowboy Ransom

For more of Barb's books, visit www.BarbHan.com.

ABOUT THE AUTHOR

Barb Han is a USA TODAY and Publisher's Weekly Bestselling Author. Reviewers have called her books "heartfelt" and "exciting."

Barb lives in Texas—her true north—with her adventurous family, a poodle mix, and a spunky rescue who is often referred to as a hot mess. She is the proud owner of too many books (if there is such a thing). When not writing, she can be found exploring new cities, on a mountain either hiking or skiing depending on the season, or swimming in her own backyard.

Sign up for Barb's newsletter at www.BarbHan.com.

Printed in Great Britain
by Amazon